RULE OF THUMB

or Death in the Family

Lauri,

I found a beat up copy, so no charge.

If you stretch the definitions — there is murder, family, genetics, chess + more.

I think I would find it hard to read, so Good Luck,

Paul

RULE OF THUMB
or Death in the Family

a mystery
without plot
character or action

by
Paul Hruban

A Shady Book
Echo
Chicago

Copyright ©1996 by Paul Hruban

All rights reserved under International and Pan-American Copyright Conventions

Shady Books
Published by Echo Books
5039 South Dorchester Avenue
Chicago, Illinois 60615

Library of Congress Card Catalog Number 96-90849

ISBN 0-9655751-1-X (Trade paper)
ISBN 0-9655751-0-1 (Limited paper)

First Trade Edition

Originally published in a Limited, Numbered, Paperback Edition

Printed in the United States of America

1 2 3 4 5 6 7 8 9 10

This is a work of fiction.
The characters and events are entirely imaginary.

Prologue

"Hi Mike!
   Just finished your manuscript and I've got to be honest in telling you that I think it's a long way from publishable.
   While I found the dialogue amusing, the characters are not fleshed out enough and the 'plot' takes a very long time to thicken. Whodunit comes out of left field - the mystery critics will jump all over that. But keep writing - your dialogue flows very smoothly."
Nancy Connor

"Hey Mike, okay, Nancy sure, but I wouldn't show that thing to George if I were you."
Brian Carter

"Dear Michael,
   I am sorry to say that as far as I can detect you have here no plot (purpose?) character, or action. You do not have a first draft even. Perhaps in the last hundred pages the pace picks up a little. Until then you are simply writing items that you think have a little verisimilitude. because they are close to what you have

observed Most authors have cautioned against this technique.

What you have: a suitably gruesome, obscene, and mysterious murder scene. Never explained. An excellent title. Better without the article. A potenetially great background. By which I mean the Company Town. It could be developed through the bars. (you might be better with just one) and the bookstore but I do not think you have done so. If I were commenting on a first draft I would strongly urge a prologue setting the scene and building suspense:

Scrolls commemorate   The City Grey Shall Never Die   Black and White Shoulder to Shoulder against the Lower Classes   The First Self-Sustaining Chain Reaction.... A man in a white coat came from the intrigues of Mittel Europa to deliver scholia to this enclavwe. Wxxx   He died in a urinal. What memorial shall be poste? Where?

Your reliance on dialogue has my sympathy and , unfortunately my encouragement. I still believe in it. However the spoken word must come from a physically visualized character. Readers must see it beng said. ..not just hear it. If you will look at a Shakespearian or Mamet play you will see that some speeches are long. An exchange of quips establishes nothing except that the charzcters are quippers. You did create an erie final dialogue between Mike and the killer...... Whether it is art or accidnnt depends on what is not available to your readers.

I was probably stupid to offer to read Rule. I am slightly glad I did because it reinforces my knowledge of your Czech persistent stubborness.

If you are serious about writing I suggest the following exercise; Write up the scene of Mike and the witches as a completely self-contained short story.....Is Mike really superstitious? Why? What are the other speakers really like? What does the bookstore look like to Mike?

A Friend."

Prof. Dr. George Goodgame

"Dear Mister Rek,

George, Professor Goodgame, passed your manuscript on to me, and I have to say ... I loved your novel. You have a rich imagination that starts with the observables of your own life as raw material and from them via the artifices of the life of the mind, creates intricate, multidimensional structures imbued with humor and pathos.

I could offer some editorial suggestions that might affect marketability and reader accessibilty, but I sense you are not looking for such input, at this time, from this direction. Regardless, you have done a thing to be proud of, and I definitely hope you will continue to write."
Professor Katya Clovek

"Dear Mr R-
Sorry, but this isn't working for me."
Kazimir Polanski

"You're a writer. I know those kind of people and I don't like them. They're misogynistic, snoopy, know-it-alls."
Caitlin O'Boyle

"You need a chase scene at the end."
Tony Grata

"You are not old enough to write a mystery, perhaps a coming-of-age novel, but not a mystery."
Ernest Buchannon

"Indeed, I am afraid the Anthropology Department may be entertaining a law suit here. This should be great fun."
Prof. John Pasteelle

"Sorry Mike, Penelope, her highness, won't let Woody stock the book. Too politically incorrect and all that."
Andrew McCaffarree

"Young man, I am extremely displeased with the way you portrayed our establishment, to say the least."
Robin Hooden

"Atleast you tried, Mike, that's what counts."
Bonney Heaney

"Magda say is good book."
Petr Prst

Chapter 1

Mike Rek blinked as his eyes focused on the clock. "The crack of noon, just like I pictured it," he muttered. He lit a cigarette and grudgingly realized that he hadn't set either alarm clock. There were forty minutes to get to work, and walking there would take twenty. He decided to skip breakfast and put three spoonfuls of instant coffee in a mug. He let the hot water run in the bathroom, then filled the mug and pretended it was coffee. It failed to fool his stomach, which groaned with acid. He frowned and dressed. He combed his hair and mustache, carefully parting them down the middle.

He hit the street, squinting at the sun through the trees, and wishing the trees hadn't been so eager to give up their leaves. He decided to take the usual route, down 55th until he hit the park at Kenwood. Then cut through Nichols Park, and over to Echo Books on 53rd and Kimbark. He plodded along slowly, hoping the walk would clear his head. As he passed the Monoxide Island apartment complex and approached Dorchester, he spotted Professor John Pasteelle at the corner. He thought about crossing the street, but the professor smiled and waved him over.

"Top of the morning to you." John said.

"I wish it were. By my watch, it's got to be afternoon." Mike replied.

"Afternoon, beautiful Sunday, don't you think? Perfect day for a stroll in our fine neighborhood."

"It's sunny, I'll give you that."

They walked together on 55th street.

"It's such a pleasant day." John said.

"What's so wonderful about Hyde Park?" Mike asked.

"Why, it's such an ethnically diverse community, perhaps the most in all Chicago. Beyond that, it's the home of our most esteemed University of Chicago."

"Yeah, it's integrated all right, like a gumbo of the weird tolerating the weirder, and each secretly knowing they're the weirdest. The U of C, that's the okra, the sticky mucilage that gooes up the whole works."

"My, aren't we full of piss and vinegar today?"

"What's that supposed to mean?"

"Well, I suppose Hyde Park could use a bowling alley."

They neared Kenwood, "This is where I turn." Mike said.

"Are you working today?" John asked.

"Yeah, I always do, same old same old, Sunday to Friday, one to eight."

"You'll be glad to know that Zoltan Gyula is speaking tomorrow, that certainly should improve your spirits."

"What's a Zoltan Gyula?"

John winced, "See you later."

"Later."

Mike took the longest winding path through Nichols Park that he could find. To his regret Echo Books was still there. He walked in. To the left, behind the counter, Brian Carter, the day manager, ran the cash register. Mike passed by Brian and parked his jacket behind the counter.

"Good morning Mike."

"Afternoon Brian."

"I see you've been trying to live up to your family name, again." Brian said.

"You mean Rek as in Veeck?" Mike asked.

"Yep."

"It was one of those wild night's at the Roost, guess maybe I might have had that one six-pack too many, if you know what I mean."

"You know, sometimes I wish I still had your tolerance for the stuff. Not today though, that's for sure."

"You seen the boss?"

"Ernie, he's in back with the Prsts."

"Firsts?"

"No, he's not working the first editions. It just rhymes with first. He's with the landlords, Peter and Magda Prst."

"And probably working himself into another tizzy, trying to provide them 'good service'."

"What's so bad about good service? Can you think of a better way to compete with the chains?"

"But we don't provide good service. Do we special order books? Mail books? Wrap gifts? Hold signings or readings? Send out a newsletter? No, no and no, and no, no and no!"

"We are friendly, most of the time. We talk to the customers," Brian offered defensively.

"Yeah, that's just it, that's personal service. That's not the same as good service. Personal service, sure. Good service, no."

"I guess " Brian said.

"So what is it about Prst and his wife that makes Ernie so nervous?"

"Peter and Magda? He could be late on the rent again."
"Maybe they're just making sure we didn't burn the place down."
"Funny, Mike. Who knows, but maybe they're actually looking for books, it happens some times. In any case, they usually buy something."
"That's true, Pete usually buys those westerns and Magda that self-help kind of stuff."
"Yep."
"Do you think they actually read them?"
"Who knows. I know I don't care. Besides, if people had to read every book they bought, we'd be out of business."
"You want me to take the register?"
"Yep, I've got to price those remainders for the DAF book sale."
"Daft book sale?"
"Department of Anthropology Family."
"Okay, I think I get you now."
Mike took over the register and kept his eye out for a tall, bald and bearded guy named Ernie. A few minutes later, Ernie appeared from behind the self-help section. As he approached the counter, Mike smelled disdain in the air. "Good afternoon," Ernie said.
"If you say so." Mike replied.

"You look more tired than you usually do on Sundays."

"Hard work and no pay."

"I believe the correct expression is 'All work and no play', and you appear to have done more than your share of the latter."

"Yeah, that's it."

"Where is Brian?"

"In the back, pricing the anthro stuff."

"Speaking of the annual Department of Anthropology Family book sale, would you be interested in attending with Brian?"

"Yeah, sure, but who's going to watch the store?"

"Excellent. I will take the shift. Frankly, I cannot stand anthropologists. They are so tolerant and so understanding of any other culture but their own."

"Brian says that those anthro women are worldly-wise, studying those primitive practices, if you know what I mean."

"I wish him luck with the she-devils."

"Well, I'm safe, I already got my 'she who must be obeyed'."

"Yes, relationships are exhausted by the young and the foolish."

"Hey, don't give up hope. Someday you'll find some one out there."
"I am afraid Echo Books takes all my time and more."
"Maybe you're already. . . ."
"Happy loving couples," Ernie interrupted, glancing down the aisle at the Prsts. "Petr and Magda Prst appear to have made their selections. Mike I want you to do your best to humor them, and minimally, at least try to be polite."
"Sure boss."
Magda scanned the bargain books by the front door and Petr approached the register.
"Hey friend, how goes it with you?" Petr asked.
"Hi Pete. Maybe one too many last night." Mike said.
"Yes. I see you with the young ladies last night."
"So how's it going with you these days?"
"Stupid childrens make me angry."
"What kids?"
"Kids in my buildings."
"What'd they do now?"
"They sing song. 'Petr, pumpkins eater. . . . '"
"That's just one of those silly nursery rhymes."

"'... had wife and could not beat her, put her in pumpkin shell and then he beats her all to.... '"

"They're just kids."

"Maybe. Maybe someday I get angry and I bang some heads together."

"Kids."

"See what I buy for wife," Petr said and handed Mike the book he was holding, *The Complete Self-Defense Guide to Small Arms for Women*.

"Life in the big city can be dangerous."

"Too many democrats on street. I not always home and she no like my shotgun. So we pick out today and pick it up tomorrow. I feel better, she feel better."

Mike looked around and noticed that Ernie was listening in. Magda moved towards the register and handed her husband *The Road Less Traveled* and *The People of the Lie*. Mike began to ring up their books.

"So how's John doing these days?" Mike asked Magda.

"Our son, yes?" She turned to Petr and he nodded. "Jan, we sent him to the old country for his graduation from high school present. Now he may witness the Independence Day," Magda said.

"And protect Slovakia from those Hungarians, they get big ideas!" Petr said with a snort.

Magda gave Petr a look of dismissive disgust, but didn't argue. Mike rang up the books. Magda took their bag and they left. Ernie reappeared from the Social Science aisle.
"Well done." Ernie said.
"Wasn't easy. I never have understood the thing some folks have for guns." Mike said.
"Which is probably a blessing, given your taste for barley and hops."
"Yeah, could be trouble. Could be trouble for Pete too. Nothing like one too many guns in the family."
"For myself, I never have understood how all the Slovaks became Republicans, or why they think all African-Americans are Democrats. After all, Mayor Cermak was a Democrat."
"I thought Cermak was Czech, not Slovak."
"Well, I hope all those ethnic differences do not cause trouble for the Prsts."
"They're both Slovaks."
"I understand that, but while they both may be Slovakian, I believe that Magda is from a Hungarian family."
"Ah, I wouldn't worry about it Ernie. Those immigrant couples, they're are all survivors, otherwise they couldn't have made it over here."

"I hope so. I am going to do some second-pricing in the back room."

"Okay, if I change the radio station?"

"You can, but *Under My Thumb* is a Rolling Stones classic."

"Sure is. But the Bears game is on, and I got them losing to Green Bay in the Roost pool."

"You should never bet against the home team."

"They never win when I bet for them."

"Gambling is a vice in either case."

"Sometimes it takes a little vice to add a little spice, especially if it's a dull game."

"Do what ever you like, I will be in the back."

Mike switched radio stations, as Ernie went to his office. Half-time, and the game with Green Bay was tied at ten. Mike settled into the slow Sunday routine. He rang up the customers and first-priced books. There were five piles of books to be priced. He looked each one up on the computer and marked the price in the book. If it wasn't on the computer, he marked the book "OP". Ernie or Brian would decide on the final price. Mike smirked each time the Bears scored. The Bears beat the Packers 30-10 and Mike tuned in the country station.

At four o'clock, Ernie and Brian emerged from the back.

"So, Mike, Ernie tells me you're tagging along for the DAF sale." Brian said.

"Yeah, sounds like it should be fun." Mike said

"Okay then, I'll pick you up at eight."

"Uh, that's a little early for me, couldn't we make it later?"

"Sure, eight-fifteen then."

"And Mike, I am more than a little concerned, I suspect Kaitlin O'Boyle's erudition may be insufficient. Let me know if you find any evidence that would confirm my suspicion." Ernie said.

"Sure Ernie, I'll keep an eye on Kate. See you guys later." Mike said.

"And I'll see you tomorrow morning." Brian said.

"Mind the store." Ernie said.

An hour and a half later, Kate strode in with a beaming smile.

"Have you heard the news, it's simply fantastic, it's almost unbelievable?" Kate said.

"Yeah, what is it? That it's Sunday and you're a half hour late again."

Kate shook her head and handed Mike a copy of the University of Chicago student newspaper, The Chicago Maroon. She had folded it over on page five. "It's right here," she said pointing to the ad.

The University of Chicago Committee on Comparative
Justice
The University of Chicago Law School
The University of Chicago Divinity School
The University of Chicago Department of Anthropology
Announce

The First Annual Bela Tuzeman Lecture

Zoltan Gyula
Professor of Grammar, Rhetoric and Logic
University of Bologna

(JUST)ICE
Destructuring the Origin of the Dark Arts
in the Transylvanian Alps
during the Age of the Angevines 1301-1382

Monday October 25 Noon
Reception following
James Henry Breasted Hall
The Oriental Institute
1155 East 58th Street

"So what's the big deal?" Mike asked.
"He was the best student Bela Tuzeman ever had." Kate said.
"Who cares."
"Come on Mike, he founded destructuralism."
"I suppose that's suppose to mean something to me."
"History of Religions is Mircea Eliade, right?"
"Yeah, so."
"History of Comparative Justice?"
"The gnome guy."
"Bela Tuzeman."
"Whatever."
"When you think of structuralism, you think of Claude Levi-Strauss."
"I suppose."
"Deconstruction is Jacques Derrida."
"I guess."
"So, when you think of destructuralism, you think of Zoltan Gyula."
"Isn't that that critical stuff."
"You remember his book, *Eros, Ecstasy, Death: Destructuring the Gnostic Hermeneutic.*"
"We never have that one in for long."
"Everybody's excited."
"I know one guy that's not."

"You should go to the lecture, it might broaden your horizons. Maybe if you took advantage of what the U has to offer, you wouldn't be such a grouch."

"I take advantage of the U of C, I sell them books, don't I?"

"I'm sure Ernie would let you come in late."

"Can't. I'm doing the DAF with Brian."

"The Anthro Family sale. I almost forgot. I should go, there might be some good Marxism, feminism or Irish history."

"Still haven't figured out what to major in, I see."

"Maybe I'll combine everything into a General Studies in the Humanities," Kate answered and asked, "Have you decided when you're going to finish your incompletes?"

"Heads up, here comes the good witch."

"Mrs. Mondevi."

A small, slender hunched-over woman shuffled toward the counter. Her hands trembled slightly as she carefully placed two books in front of Mike.

"I see you're reading Annie Rice this week." Mike said.

"Yes, I think I will," she said, with a grandmotherly smile, marred only by her dead and stained teeth. "I read *The Mummy* last week and found

it rather humorous, so I have decided to try her earlier work. Have you read *The Interview with the Vampire* or *The Vampire Lestat*?"
"I read her trilogy about a princess, and that was kind of funny, but the vampire books, no, I haven't." Mike said.
"My roommate really likes her." Kate added. "But the angst and ennui, they sort of depress her."
"So you have read the books?" Mrs. Mondevi asked.
"Only the first hundred pages of the Interview." Kate said.
"Why dear?"
"I got the message, it's boring being a vampire."
"Do not worry dear. I am too old to allow stories to depress me, and besides, I find they all bore me." She reassured Kate. "But what does raise my hackles is those messages you put in your books."
"What messages?" Kate asked.
"Sorry about that." Mike said and turned to Kate, "She's taking about the 'Forsake Satan' and 'Jesus loves you' slips."
"Yes those!" Mrs. Mondevi said.
"We would never do that." Kate assured her.

"That's not us, that's the Jesus Defense League, over on campus, they're trying to save our customers." Mike said.

"The JDL sneaks in on Sundays and puts those slips in any book they consider the slightest bit anti-Christian." Kate added.

"They must figure that all good Christians are in church." Mike said.

"You know, I have seen them and I just assumed they worked for the bookstore." Mrs. Mondevi said.

"Yeah, well, they don't! You ever see them again in here, let me know and I'll . . . ah, let them know they are no longer welcome in Echo Books, how's that?" Mike said.

"I certainly will do just that." Mrs. Mondevi said.

Kate handed her the newspaper, "You've heard about the lecture tomorrow?"

Taking her reading glasses out of her purse, Mrs. Mondevi studied the advertisement. Folding the glasses back into their case, she handed the paper back to Kate. "Thank you."

"So you're going to go, I can tell."

"I tried to read that fellow's book once, Sex and Death or some silliness."

"*Eros, Ecstasy, Death.*" Kate offered.

"Yes, some such. Unfortunately, I have a great deal of trouble understanding anything that the young man has written."

"It's destructuralism."

"I can not even understand the title of his speech, but I'm sure scholars like yourself will find it most rewarding."

"But it's Zoltan Gyula." Kate protested.

"Thank you very much dear," Mrs. Mondevi smiled as she collected her bag and left the store.

"Kate, you know, if you could scare all the customers off with that Gyula guy, we could close up early tonight." Mike said.

"Very funny."

"Why don't you clip that ad and post it on the front door." Mike suggested.

"I think I will do just that." Kate said and taped the ad at eye level to the middle of the glass door.

"So Kate, if it's okay with you, I'm going to do some shelving and straightening?"

"Every night I take the register and you hide in back. Any other profound questions?"

"Nah, just let me know if anyone comes in with books to sell," Mike said and escaped to the rear of the store.

Earlier, Ernie had pulled some of the older books off the new arrivals table and added them to others on the preshelving shelves. Mike sorted the preshelving into stacks for Literature, Philosophy, Social Science and History. There were a few more odd sections, including Mike's favorite, Humor? Etc. As he shelved the books, he looked at the pictures for something worth skimming. After he finished shelving the major sections, he put aside *How Real Is Real?*.

Then he straightened the shelves and pulled a few misshelved books. He took Asimov's *The Genetic Code* out of Science Fiction and reshelved it in Natural History. He spotted *Memoirs of Hadrian* in Literature and put it back in Ancient Mediterranean History. When he was finished, he picked up *How Real Is Real?*, sat on the corner of the New Arrivals table, and began to thumb through the book.

Thirty minutes later, there was a tap on his shoulder, "Ahem. Work to do," Kate said.

"I was just checking if this was suitable for our customers." Mike said.

"I'm sure, but there's some guy up front that wants to sell some books, and he asked for you."

"Why did I ever agree to become a buyer?"

"I don't care, just come up front."

Mike straightened himself out, practiced his confident and self-assured facial expressions, nodded sincerely and walked towards the front.
"Well hello, Dr. Weir, how are you?" Mike asked.
"I am just fine, how are you?" Dr. Weir asked.
"Not bad myself, considering. Books to sell?"
"Yes. We received more review copies."
"Very good, let's have a look."
Dr. Weir hefted the boxes of books on to the top of the bookshelves that served as the book-buying table. Mike took the books out and sorted them into three stacks. Starting at the bottom he began to measure each stack with the width of his thumb.
"Two dollars an inch, same as last time okay?" Mike asked.
"Yes, of course. I see you still haven't found your ruler." Dr. Weir said
"No. But the thumb's about an inch wide and it's easier this way anyhow."
"Where did you learn that, not at the University I assume."
"Nah. I read that here."
"Read carefully."

The stacks were 15, 11 and 22 thumbs tall. "I'm coming up with 95 bucks, that sound about right?" Mike asked assuredly.
"More than enough to cover the postal expenses of the journal."
Mike moved to the register and rang up the book buy. He filled out the receipt form and handed it to Dr. Weir, for him to sign. "So how's your baby doing these days, it's Brain Research isn't it?" Mike asked.
"No, that's another journal," Dr. Weir sighed as he signed. "Our journal is *META KEPHALOS: An Interdisciplinary Critical Inquiry into the Human Brain.*"
"Would you publish something by Professor Gyula?" Kate asked.
"Of course, he has never submitted an article for publication, but hypothetically, I would have to say we are not as interdisciplinary as we might be." Dr. Weir answered.
"Well here's the money." Mike said.
"Thank you, I must be going."
"Bunch of hypocrites." Kate groused as he left the store.
"I kind of like the guy myself. Brings in a lot of weird stuff and never complains about our price." Mike said.

"Okay, then he's an ignoramus."

Mike shrugged and went back to the book buy. He started to process the new books he'd bought. He marked each with Ernie's secret code, which revealed where the book was bought, when, for how much, who did the buy and where it should be shelved.

"So anything good?" Kate asked.

"It's mostly symposiums, proceedings from conferences, colloquiums and seminars, stuff that only sells to the people that went to them."

"So why did you give him all that money?"

"There are a couple good Harvard and MIT titles, all bio stuff. Besides, a lot of those U of C types go to the conferences."

"Any gender or cultural studies or Irish history?"

"Nah, I told you, nothing you'd be interested in."

Mike finished coding the books and sorted them into three piles, bargain books, marginal and solid titles. Tomorrow, Ernie or Brian could decide what went on the bargain table and what went into regular stock. Mike took the stacks to the back room and then went back to shelving books.

When all of the big sections were done, Mike started on the how-to books, what Ernie had labeled as Reference and Recreation. It was one of the smaller sections near the front of the store. Behind the bookcases, across from the register, Mike could hear the conversation at the cash register.

A tall, slender man entered the store. He removed his beret and approached Kate. He said, "Pardon. Where will I look for works of Habermas?"

"Harpo Marx, let's see. If we have anything, it should be in the Performing Arts. It's right over there." Kate said pointing to the section ten feet away.

Befuddled, the man walked to the section that Kate had pointed to and began to survey the books. Mike waited two minutes and then quietly approached the customer.

"Ah, excuse me, were you looking for Habermas?" Mike whispered.

"Yes. Strange place for him. Perhaps his *Theory of Communicative Action*, yes?" He replied.

"Normally, he's shelved in Philosophy or Social Science. Let me show you where Philosophy is." Mike said and led him half way down the left hand aisle. "Social Science is just over on the other side," Mike added.

"Thank you sir." The man said.

Mike returned to shelving the how-to books. He saved Humor? Etc. for last. He thumbed through Prof. Arnold Ehret's *Mucusless Diet Healing System* and decided it wasn't for him. As closing time approached,

he finished shelving and straightening, and returned to the front counter. Once there, he finished the look-ups from the afternoon.
"Mike I saw you talk to that guy." Kate said.
"Maybe I did." Mike said.
"What did you say to him?" Kate asked.
"Nothing."
"You told him to look for the Marx Brothers in Philosophy, didn't you?"
"Well."
"You've got a twisted sense of humor."
"You could look at the Marx Brothers as social philosophers or social critics, that kind of thing."
"Some day I'm going to tell Ernie about your silly pranks."
"Actually, all I said to him was that he looked like a intellectual guy with broad interests, and that we happen to have a particularly good philosophy section, right now."
"Sure," Kate said doubtfully. "Well, he did end up buying a half dozen high-powered books on German social criticism. So I guess your prank worked."
"See."
"Never mind."
"I tell you sometimes I can read those customers like a book."

"Are you going to Robert's Roost tonight?"
"Yeah. Nancy picked up Ken's afternoon shift at the Roost and got off at seven. I'm supposed to met her there after work."
"I'm meeting my roommate there. Mind if I walk with you?"
"Hyde Park by night. No problem."
"Thanks."
"I thought you guys went to Jimmy's."
"She said she wanted to get away from all the students."
"It's almost eight."
"Let's close up."

Chapter 2

"It's so polluted in here." Kate said.
"What'd you expect?" Mike said.
"There's too much noise, too many people and it's too smoky."
"The Roost is a bar."
"How can anyone stand it?"
"It's not like it's a health club."
"Do you see Brigid anywhere?"
"I can't see anything through the miasma."
"Funny."
"Looks like a table of students over there in the back."
"There?"
"No, there, in the back by the kitchen."
"There she is and she brought Marti with her."
"If you say so."
"Thanks for walking me, see ya later."
"Later."
Mike surveyed the bar. Every bar stool was taken, most of the tables and even the booth by the door. Mike spotted Brian at the bar.
"Hi Brian." Mike said.

"You closed up?" Brian asked.

"Yeah."

"Time for me to go."

"Hey, you don't have to go. I promise I won't even mention the bookstore."

"It's not that, it's just that it's always close to nine by the time you get here."

"Past your bedtime?"

"I need my beauty sleep."

"Otherwise you'd be a Veeck."

"Exactly." Brian said and then shrugged. "Look, it's crowded, why don't you take my seat. These two fine gentlemen can keep you company."

"Thanks," Mike said and they traded places.

"Why don't you guys tell Mike, about our distinguished visitor." Brian said.

"It would be my pleasure." Professor Pasteelle volunteered.

"Just a load of nonsense." Professor Goodgame said.

"Well, then, I leave you in good hands. I'll pick you up at eight." Brian said.

"I thought we agreed on eight-thirty." Mike protested.

"Right, and try to remember not to have that 'one-too-many'," Brian said to Mike. Then he turned to the others and said "Good night folks, I'll be seeing you."

Mike gestured to the bartender without success.

"So what's going on here? It's so busy, I may never get a beer." Mike said.

"It's that Italian charlatan, that's what." Professor Goodgame said.

"Easy George. He is one of the founding fathers of destructuralism." Professor Pasteelle cautioned.

"Kaz, Kaz, can I get I beer down here!" Mike said.

"Hold your horses. Can't you see I'm busy." Kazimir shouted.

"When you get a chance then." Mike said, and turned to the professors, "It's never busy on Sunday."

Kaz came down the bar. "Old Style Mike?" He said.

"Yeah, that'd be fine, thanks."

Kaz brought the beer and Mike paid for it.

"Yes, Kazimir. I would like an Augsburger and see if George would like anything." Pasteelle said.

Kaz looked at George.

"I'll take a stein on John."

Kaz went to get the beers.

"Say, George, have you seen Nancy? She was supposed to get off at seven" Mike asked.

"She was definitely here earlier."

Kaz returned with the Augsburger and the stein.

"Kaz, did Nancy work for Ken today?"

"She sure did." Kaz said.

"What time did she leave?"

"I can't say just yet."

"It's not like it's a big deal."

"Could be. She's over in the booth, sitting next to the movie star."

Mike craned his neck to the left. In the center of the booth by the door was a man in a white trench coat. The booth surrounded a rectangular table and it was packed on all sides. The movie star had long white hair combed straight back, and it matched his coat. Nancy sat on his left, to his right was Magda, and across the table was the gnome drinking a Gibson.

"Thanks, I didn't spot Nancy without her cap." Mike said.

"Hey Pal, don't worry about it. I wouldn't have either, if I hadn't seen her take it off and fluff up her hair, when that guy came in." Kaz said.

"She didn't."

"You got something there, try not to blow it this time."

"Thanks Kaz," Mike said turning to John. "So who's the movie star?"

"You mean the center of attraction in the booth?"

"The guy with the white hair."

"Zoltan Gyula is in town to give the Tuzeman lecture."

"That's Gyula?"

"Yes, Bela's star pupil. Did you know he studied under me once, as well?" John said.

"Bela? You mean the gnome, the guy drinking a Gibson?" Mike asked.

"The creator of comparative justice." George said.

"So the gnome retires and his chickens come home to roost." Mike said.

"They are merely showing respect to their mentor." John corrected.

"So why the crowd?" Mike asked.

"Zoltan took Bela's method and came up with destructuralism. I know it is hard to believe, but it happens." John said.

"Stupid nonsense." George said.

"And I suppose postmodern poetry is different?"

"They invent theoretical frameworks to prove what they thought was true when they were born."

"I thought all professors did that." Mike said.

"Don't step into something that you know nothing about." George said.

"Okay. But what do the women find so exciting about this Gyula guy?" Mike asked.

"He must have learned a lot from the Latins." George said.

"Come now, George, a forty year old man with a full head of striking white hair and blue eyes as soft as a mother's kiss." John said.

"Lucky for Hyde Park his wife is coming in tomorrow night." George added.

"That's a relief." Mike said.

"I'm sure if he wants to get lucky tonight. . . ."

"Thanks, George," Mike said, and turned to John. "What's Gyula doing at the Roost, anyway?"

"Oh, Bela was worried that he'd be mobbed by students at Jimmy's, and since most students are scared of this place, he thought that wouldn't be a problem here."

"I don't think the plan worked." Mike said.

"Zoltan's happy, he's surrounded by women." George added.

"Yes. He loves the ladies." John said.

"Or loves being loved." George said

"Nah, he's in love with himself, like a movie star." Mike said.

"That's what I just said." George objected.

"Regardless, he appears to be quite taken by Nancy." John said.

"I can see that. He ought to stick to Magda, she's more his age and I bet she speaks Hungarian." Mike said.

"Funny, I always thought they were Slovaks." George said.

"Not to worry Mike, you know how it goes. When you're doing the flirting it's innocent fun, of course, but when your partner does, it's the gravest of sins." John said.

"She still shouldn't look at him like that." Mike muttered.

"If it makes you feel any better, take a look at that guy, half-way down the bar." George said.

Mike looked down the bar and saw Petr scowling at his beer.

"You see, he's not happy either." George said.

"Pete probably just got a bad beer."

"Come now Mike, you know as well as I that, after a couple beers, Peter is usually a friend to any one that will listen. Acquiantance and stranger alike." John said.

"Yeah, he's not his usual self." Mike said.

"So you see, you're not the only who's less than pleased with the appearance of that Latin Lover."

"Nice try George."

"Then what about Mel Hastscort?" George asked.

"The resident stud, what about him?" Mike asked.

"Malcolm Hastscort III looks very distracted. You know, it must be hard. The best looking guy in the place and he finally has some competition." John said.

"Must be hard being the big fish in a small pond." Mike said.

"Personally, I rather enjoy watching that Don Juan squirm." George said.

"You think Janet is safe?" Mike asked.

"She never gets into any trouble that she hasn't planned on." George said.

"You know, that's true, I never have seen her in a situation where she wasn't in control." John said.

"So Nancy should be safe tonight."

"Destructuring your question Mike, I would have to say no." John said.

"Exactly what is destructuring?"

"Applying the critical methodology of destructualism."
John said.

"So what's this destucturalism stuff?"

"I will try to make it simple for you. Michael, imagine a poem, a novel, a legal code, or any text, as a skeleton. The destucturalist analysis would dictate that you separate the meat from the bones. Ignore the bones, the structure, and concentrate on the meat, the muscle, the power, the motive force." John explained.

"Too deep for me." Mike said.

"Very well. What did you study?" John asked.

"It's a long story but political science." Mike said.

"Let me rephrase. I suspect that Gyula would argue that you should ignore the legislative, executive and judiciary, and concentrate on the military and the financial." John said.

"I still don't get you."

"He means that if you have guns and money, you don't need lawyers." George said.

"Yeah, well I don't got lawyers, guns or money."

"Yes, yes. I've never thought of you as empowered." John said.

"I can beat anybody at 'Deer Hunter'." Mike said.

"Now I don't get it." John said.

"He's talking about that pin-bowling machine." George said.

"Mike, why don't you go over there," John said, pointing to the video games, "and see if can't beat some aliens." John said.
"I don't like the video machines. Who needs creatures chasing after you, especially when you've been drinking." Mike said.
"Then you might consider the bowling machine." George said.
"Nah, I think I'll try my luck on 'Deer Hunter'." Mike said, as he stood up.
"Good luck." George said.
"He should be lucky at cards." John said to George.
"What?"
"Next time remind me never to ask you guys about postmodern poetry." Mike said.
"Good night, Michael." Both professors said.
Mike walked down the bar and, nodding to the regulars. On the right at the end of the bar were two pinball machines and four video games. Tony Grata, an off-duty cop, was playing Speed Queen, one of the pinball machines. Mike watched Tony play his last ball.
"So what's the deal?" Mike asked Tony.
"You mean the new machine?" Tony asked.
"Yeah, of course I mean the new machine, what else would I mean." Mike said.

"Seems nobody was playing Deer Hunter."

"It was my favorite machine."

"Except you."

"Just when I was getting good."

"So Robin had this new one put in. Kind of a Halloween thing I guess, seeing as how Halloween is next Saturday."

"Twisted Sisters?"

"It's about witches."

"Double, double, toil and trouble." The Twisted Sisters machine chanted.

"Don't tell me it's one of those talking machines." Mike said.

"Yeah, I hate those fake computer voice things too." Tony said.

"Whatever happened to the old fashioned bells and pops?" Mike asked.

"Most machines have the fake voices these days."

"You try it yet?"

"Yeah, it's not so bad."

"Maybe I'll give it a try."

"Be my guest, you know you're going to anyway. Just don't say I didn't warn you."

"You didn't warn me."

"I said. . . ."

"Might as well try it, Nancy's acting busy, so all I got to lose is quarters."

"I noticed, what's the deal?"

"I don't know, that hot shot professor or something I said. I never can tell what'll set her off."

"I think I'll give Queenie here one more try."

Tony slipped a quarter into Speed Queen and Mike put four quarters into Twisted Sisters.

"I'll get you, my pretty, and your little dog." Twisted Sisters crowed.

"No you won't, and besides I got cats." Mike answered.

Mike pulled back the firing pin and stroked the first ball into the game. The ball came down the third slot and lit an eye. It bounced off of the black cats, hit a broomstick and then went straight down the middle.

"Fire burn and caldron bubble." Twisted Sisters said.

"Yeah, well, you're going to be in double trouble yourself, when I get through with you." Mike said.

"Quit talking to the machine," Tony said. "You're distracting me."

"It's better than arguing with Nancy."

"It's just a machine."

"Maybe it's a game I can win at."

"Now see what you did, I lost the ball."

"At least machines have some rules."
"Try reading them some time."
"That might help."

Mike stared at the rule card. It had something to do with black cats, broomsticks, buckets and caldrons. He couldn't make any sense out of the rules. He decided to shoot at the easiest targets, the black cats and the broomsticks. His second shot lit the eye on the left, and then bounced around between the cats and the sticks before it drained.

"Fire burn and caldron bubble."
"Yeah, I know."

He pulled back the third ball and gently eased into the center slot. The third eye lit. He shook the machine to give the ball more action. The tilt sign went on and his flippers stopped working.

"Fair is foul and foul fair."
"I tilted, so what." Mike said and turned to Tony. "Any ideas?" He asked.
"You cost me another ball." Tony said.
"Here, call somebody that cares." Mike said and handed Tony some coins.
"Thanks. Well for starters, you want to light the evil eyes."
"I did that."

"To advance the bonus you have to knock down thirteen broomsticks, or hit the four witches."

"Over here and around here?"

"Yeah."

"How do you light the special?"

"Two ways. Up this ramp you advance the bonus and if you do it five times, then it lights the special."

"What's the other way."

"It's a lot harder, you got to go up this ramp here, which isn't easy, and then drop it in the bucket. That releases all the balls and lights the special."

"What balls?"

"Every time you hit a witch it holds your ball."

"Where's the special?"

"The ruby slippers over here."

"What happens if I hit them when the special's not lit?"

"Still a good shot. It closes the one of the side drains and the post comes up in the middle."

"I could get into to this."

"I can see."

Mike turned and went to the bar and waited for Kaz. When Kaz came down to the far end, he said "A couple of Old Styles and a couple of dollars in quarters too."

"You've met the new machine, I see." Kaz said.

"Given enough time, they can be beat." Mike said.

Kaz got the beers and quarters. "Good luck Pal," he said.

Mike put the beers on the rail by the wall. He plugged in his quarters and pressed the start button.

"I'll get you, my pretty, and your little dog," chortled Twisted Sisters.

"I heard that somewhere before."

He started to play. He decided to try the shots Tony had told him about. He aimed for the witch on the left and hit it.

"Just try and keep out of my way." Twisted Sisters said.

"That's what I was thinking."

He got a new ball and hit the witch at the top of the machine.

"Never let those ruby slippers off your feet."

With a new ball, he aimed for the ramp on the left and hit the Newt.

"Eye of newt." The machine said.

He caught the ball and shot again.

"Eye of newt, toe of frog."

And again.

"Eye of newt, toe of frog, wool of bat."

He took another shot and lit the special.

"Eye of newt, toe of frog, wool of bat and tongue of dog."

He aimed for the glowing ruby slippers. The machine popped and he won a free game. "I think I'm going to like this game." Mike said to the where Tony had been.

Mike settled into the machine and practiced the different shots. Thirteen quarters, six beers and three hours later, Mike tried to drop it in the bucket. It fell in and the machine popped.

"I'm, melting." Twisted Sisters said.

"About time."

"Who'd have thought a girl like you could destroy my beautiful wickedness?"

"First off, I'm not a girl. Second, you got to wake up pretty early in the afternoon, to get one over on me. Besides you're not that bad looking compared to that happy face blonde." Mike said.

"Glinda?"

"Yeah, the one with the goofy smile."

"Hover through the fog and filthy air." Twisted Sisters said.

"Not you too."

Exhausted and drained, Mike returned to the bar. He looked around, and it was almost empty.

Sylvester, Andrew and Petr were still at the bar. Kate's table had dwindled down to two. The booth at the other end was still full.

"Kaz, a beer if you please." Mike said.

"You sure?" Kaz asked.

"Yeah."

"You were talking to the pinball machine."

"It was talking to me."

"Okay, but remember, you got to be up early tomorrow."

"Eight."

"Eight-thirty."

"Takes me a while to get dressed."

Mike turned from the bar and stepped up to Kate's table. Brigid gestured to Kate, who turned towards Mike.

"Hi Mike, I thought you were going to meet Nancy." Kate said.

"Not just yet." Mike said.

"Would you like to join us?"

"Only till Nancy is ready of course."

"Have a seat."

"Kate and I were talking about the Tuzeman lecture." Brigid said.

"I heard. Defactotumalism or something." Mike said.

"Destructuralism!" Kate corrected.
"Whatever." Mike said.
"Actually, Professor Gyula is also a very important player in the environmental movement in Eastern Europe." Brigid said.
"He's a Green too." Kate said.
"What's a green?" Mike asked.
"You know." Kate said.
"The environmentalists in Europe have their own political party." Brigid said.
"Those Eco-Mafia types should throw more parties, maybe they'd lighten up." Mike said.
"Remember, I warned you about him." Kate said.
"This is serious! Zoltan Gyula is an attaché to the Hungarian Green Party's Committee on Cultural Preservation." Brigid said.
"So, what does he do?" Mike asked.
"He played a big part in stopping that dam on the Danube that the Czechs were putting up on the border between Hungary and Slovakia." Brigid said
"The Danube Hydroelectric Project, yes, of course." Kate agreed.
"And now it won't pollute the largest source of drinking water in the region." Brigid added.

"What'd he do, blow it up and cause a flood that killed millions of people?" Mike asked.
"Don't be stupid. It wasn't finished yet." Kate said.
"No, the Hungarians don't want it built, so the Czechs decided to change the course of the Danube. They were rerouting the Danube at that point so that it only went through Slovakia." Brigid said.
"That should do the trick." Mike said.
"Then came Zoltan Gyula." Brigid said.
"Uh-oh." Mike said.
"No, wait, this is great, he dug up the border treaties." Brigid said.
"So."
"It turns out that the border between Slovakia and Hungary is the center of the navigable route of the Danube."
"So all the Slovaks would be doing is giving up land?"
"Yes, that's the beauty of it."
"The Slovaks hate him." Kate said.
"They're not the only ones." Mike said.
"Yes, of course you're envious of Professor Gyula, we all are." Brigid said.
"No, I think he's jealous because Nancy's sitting in the booth." Kate said.

"Nancy?"

"His fiancée."

"She's not my fiancée. All I said was, I thought we would get married after she got her Master's." Mike said.

"Maybe you should approach Nancy with the idea before you go and tell anybody else." Brigid suggested.

"I guess sometimes I should keep my mouth shut." Mike said.

"So you are jealous." Kate said.

"I got nothing to say." Mike said.

"Don't feel so bad, I'm sure you're not the only one." Kate said.

"There's that janitor at the bar." Brigid added.

Mike turned and looked. "That's Pete. He's not just a janitor, he owns a bunch of buildings in Hyde Park. More than you'd think, a lot of those janitors do."

"Isn't that his wife sitting next to the Professor and Nancy?" Kate asked.

"Yeah that's her."

"So you see." Brigid said.

"I see that I'm going to see what Pete thinks about the dam."

"You're leaving us?" Kate said.

"Moving to the bar, that's all."

"Well, in that case, I think Brigid and I are going to join the booth."

"Be my guest."

"There seems to be some room." Brigid said.

"Later." Mike said. He grabbed his beer, nodded and turned to the bar. There was a seat between Petr and Andrew, and Mike took it. "So, Pete, how's it going?"

"Good. How goes it with you?"

"Not so bad. Ernie late on the rent again?"

"No, he pay. But maybe you no pay?"

"I just work there."

"You right. But I buy you building too." Petr chuckled.

"No way. Old man Rowe would never sell."

"He not sell. He in home for old peoples. His son, he not like business. He sell to Petr."

"Good luck."

"Hey, you funny man. Good luck. Good luck to you. You still not pay October rent. Sunday you owe two months."

"Rowe always let me slide for a month."

"No more Rowe, maybe no more Rek."

"I can't come up with two months rent on Sunday."

"Okay. Because you good friend, I let you pay one and half."

"Thanks, but I think maybe we got bigger problems, Nancy and Magda are talking to that hotshot professor."

"Magda, she like speak Magyar sometime."

"Gyula."

"How you say? . . . Hungarian."

"Nancy doesn't know Hungarian as far as I know."

"I no either."

"So you're not worried at all by all the attention they're giving him?"

"My Magda, she know she go home with me."

"I guess there are certain advantages to being married."

"Yeah, sure, of course. Take my advice and marry that woman of yours."

"Remind me to ask her some time."

"Hey buddy, any time you need advices, come to me."

"So did you pick out a gun for Magda yet?"

"Yes. Magda like Raven .25 auto. With the chrome, lady's gun."

"Where you going to get it?"

"Buddy of mine's has shop in Cicero. He save one for me."

"Sounds good."

"I get good price too. I buy second hand, you know, used."

"Yeah."

"My wife, she no need know. Gun is gun, still kill you."

"Guess you're right."

"Of course I right."

Mike looked down and shook his head. They sipped their beers and stared at the bottles behind the bar. Andrew and Sylvester were arguing about something in the news. Mike was trying to think of another question, when he felt a tap on his shoulder. He turned to face a grinning Kate.

"I thought you might like to know that Professor Gyula is taking us all dancing." Kate said.

"At midnight on a Sunday, sure." Mike said.

"Apparently there's some function going on at the Hungarian Cultural Club."

"It had to be some place weird."

"The good thing is, you don't have to wait for Nancy."

"No."

"She drove Magda."

"I couldn't have waited anyway, I got to be up early tomorrow."

"Well, see you on Tuesday then."

"Later."

Mike looked at the booth. The only one left was the Gnome. At seventy-one, Bela Tuzeman wasn't going dancing tonight. Mike wasn't going dancing either. A student helped the Gnome with his coat. Mike turned to Petr.

"Say, I thought you said your wife was going home with you?" Mike said.

"Of course." Petr looked around the bar and said, "Where she go now. She in Ladies, I bet."

"She went to the Hungarian Cultural Club, Nancy drove her."

"Why she go there?"

"That Hungarian took them dancing."

"No."

"I wouldn't joke about something like that."

"It no good."

"You're telling me."

"I go see she not in big trouble."

"Keep an eye on Nancy while you're at it."

Petr left in a huff. Sylvester put on his knapsack and his hat and left. Kaz cleared the booth table of empty bottles and glasses. He moved down the bar and started washing glasses in front of Mike and Andrew.

"I'm being deserted." Kaz said.

"There are just the three of us left." Andrew said.

"You guys care for a drink on Robert?" Kaz asked.

"Don't tell me he's still not feeling well." Andrew said.

"Robin said his arthritis was acting up again."

"Sure, in that case I'll have a Special Export."

"Anything for you Mike?"

"I guess I'll take an Old Style." Mike said.

"Seeing as how Robert is buying," Kaz winked. "I think I'll have a shot of Wild Turkey."

"Thanks Kaz, I worked today, I can use this."

"Hey pal, talk about busy days, I had almost more than I could handle tonight."

"Yeah, well, your woman didn't go out with another guy did she?"

"So Mike, how are you doing in the pool this week?" Andrew asked.

"I had the Bears to lose. I think I already lost four games."

"Normally the winner has only two losses. My guess would be you don't have much of a chance." Andrew said.

"Are you serious about Nancy?" Kaz asked.

"She left with that Zoltan guy, didn't she?" Mike said.

"That is what I saw." Kaz said.

"Is he serious?" Andrew asked.

"Andrew, anyone ever tell you that you were a strange, alien and dog-like creature?" Mike asked.

"Oh, I've been called much worse. I was called a toad once, and at work they call me 'Professor', like I know everything, which I don't, and of course nobody could. Not since Leonardo da Vinci anyway. Talk about insulting some one, just try calling them 'Professor'." Andrew said.

"Ah, Mike, I think maybe it's time for you to call it a night." Kaz said.

"I got to get to work tomorrow." Mike said.

"I've had enough action tonight. I don't need you calling Andrew a professor." Kaz said.

"'Sides you guys are no fun."

"Good night, Mike."

"Have a safe walk." Andrew said.

"It's only a block." Mike said.

"Just get going." Kaz said.

"Okay, okay. Later guys."

Chapter 3

Mike watched the Echo Books van pull on to Cornell and stop in front of his apartment building. He put out his cigarette and walked to the used post office van. Brian slid open the door and Mike got in.
"Morning Brian."
"Mike, I hardly recognized you."
"Yeah, well, I recognized the van."
"So are you ready for a day of some real work?"
"A change of pace might be just what I need."
"When we get there, first thing we do is unload the boxes. All nineteen of them."
"That's only ten a piece."
"Yep and I can't wait until you lift one."
"You said the sale starts at ten or something."
"That's right."
"So we unload the boxes and just wait in line?"
"Of course, if you haven't had your breakfast. . .
"I had my usual."
"In that case, you want to stop for doughnuts or bagels, maybe a little coffee?"
"Nah, I'm fine "

Rule of Thumb

Brian put the van in drive and they were on their way. Brian turned left onto 55th. They drove silently passed Monoxide Island until they reached Woodlawn. Brian took a left and then a right at 58th. The traffic suddenly slowed to a crawl. They inched along.

"Hard to believe there's a line to get into the Oriental Institute at this hour." Mike said.

"Looks like the students must be protesting something again." Brian said.

"That sign over there says 'Viva Structuralism'."

"Reminds me of the old days somehow."

"There's another one over there that says 'Forsake Satan'."

"Christians, they're always causing trouble."

"It could be those Jesus people."

"The Jesus Defense League, the JDL?"

"That's right. We could finally set them straight, Echo Books-wise."

"Isn't Zoltan Gyula giving a lecture today."

"Kate was all excited."

"That must be what stirred them all up."

"What? Look that sign says 'Renounce Gyula'."

"I had a customer once that told me that Gyula was the Anti-Christ. Told me that we shouldn't sell his books. We should just buy them and burn them."

"What about the JDL?"

"There are five different seminaries in Hyde Park. What makes you think they are the JDL?"

"Hard to believe Hyde Park finally got religion."

"Now that's another question altogether."

"Then what about that other sign? Viva Structuralism."

"They're anthropologists obviously."

"That could be dangerous."

"With them you never can tell. I just hope they didn't call off the book sale."

They made their way through the noisy protesters and crossed University Avenue. Brian circled the drive in the central quadrangle, and then turned south onto a smaller quadrangle Haskell Hall, on the west side, was the home of the Anthropology Department and the site of the DAF book sale. Almost all the no-parking spots were taken. Brian finally found one on the east side.

"You wait here and watch the van. I'm going to go inside and see where Joey wants us to put the stuff." Brian said.

"Who's he?" Mike said.

"Joey Hines, the guy that runs the book sale."

"Whatever you say, boss."

Mike waited and watched the students go to their nine o'clock classes. They looked young. The

Rule of Thumb

ones going into the building on his right looked hard-edged. Harold Leonard Stuart Hall. He tried and couldn't remember which classes he had had in there. Brian came across the quadrangle with a two-wheel hand truck.

"Joey says we should bring the books in through the back door. It's on the other side in the center of the building."

"You know, sometimes I still think of myself as a student."

"They're starting to look young, aren't they?"

"With my incompletes, I figured I was in that limbo zone between undergrad and grad."

"What are you now? Twenty-eight?"

"Yeah."

"The freshmen are eighteen, that's a ten year difference."

"So?"

"Give it ten years. When you get to be my age, you'll understand."

"Thanks, Dad. I can't remember if I had any classes in there." Mike said, pointing to Stuart Hall.

"I doubt it."

"I could have."

"Read the sign."

"I did, Harold Leonard Stuart Hall."

"And the rest of it."

"Oh, right, the Graduate School of Business."

"The U of C keeps those B-schoolers segregated and pampered. They even have a separate Alumni office and believe me, it brings in the big bucks."

"That would explain why those students all have dollar signs carved in the diamonds of their eyes."

"Maybe to you."

"They're hard-boiled."

"Let's unload the truck. Here, you take the hand truck, I got from Joey, and I'll use ours."

Brian rolled up the back of the van. He climbed in and started stacking boxes on the sidewalk in piles of four.

"Why's Ernie still using those old Baker and Taylor boxes?" Mike asked.

"He's a pack rat." Brian answered.

"Cheap, you mean. They must be twenty years old."

"Probably six. Probably left over from when he worked at Prairie City. Check the address on the side."

"Prairie City Bookshop. Didn't you used to work there?"

"Enough talk, quit stalling. Do four boxes per load, five if you're feeling macho."

"Stalling, huh. You want macho, you got it."

Mike loaded six boxes on to his hand truck. Brian loaded four and shook his head. Mike had to use one hand to control the top box because it rested above the top of the hand truck. When they reached the back entrance to Haskell, Mike was triumphantly strained.

"Let's prop open the doors with boxes." Brian said.

Brian propped open the first set of double doors. Mike propped open the second.

"There's no way I can get that hand truck up those stairs." Mike said.

"No? A big strong man like you?"

"These books have got to weigh close to three hundred pounds."

"In that case, why don't you put them by this handicap lift thing, like I am."

"Sounds good to me."

"I thought it might."

"You know how to work this thing?"

"That's Joey's problem."

"Another load should do the trick."

"Be my guess."

They circled around Haskell and crossed the quad.

"Let's see, we got nine left, if you take six, that means I take three." Brian said.

"I think I'll try five this time."
"Okay. But let's speed it up. There's already a line out the door."
"Who would get in line at this hour?"
"Dealers of course."
"Like Romanowski?"
"Romanowski, sure, John and his wife, Jack and Rodney from Sartoris, Zippy, and what's his name, Adam Yaecker or something."
"Yaeckel."
"Just look at the line, and I'm sure they're not the only ones."
"Well, in that case, let's get these bargain books in there."
"They're not the bargain books."
"General stock?"
"Remainders. He placed a large order with Daedalus just for this sale."
"Why?"
"Cover the cost of whatever we buy."
"We got a whole lot of books to buy then."
"We're not going to sell everything and we're going to buy even less."

They loaded the hand trucks and brought them to the back doors at the center of Haskell. Hines was holding the door.

"Glad to see you guys from Echo Books could make it this year." Joey said.

"What'd you mean, we've made it every year. At least for the last five years." Brian said.

"I saved a spot for you on the first floor, fifteen steps on the right side."

"Great. Joey, this is Mike Rek, he's supposed to help me out today. Mike, this is Joey Hines, the guy I was telling you about."

"Pleased to meet you." Mike said

"Welcome to the Anthro family." Joey said.

"Thanks. A spare family might come in handy sometime."

"So how's the selection look this year?" Brian said.

"Quite good. All the usual suspects are participating. There's Prairie City Bookshop, Powell's, the U of C Press, AJS and CA, the other Anthro journals and of course the Anthro Family." Joey said.

"Anything special to look out for?"

"There is a student, he works for the U of C Bookstore, he's selling a lot of high-powered destructualism."

"What's his number?"

"17, and they should move fast, with the Gyula man himself in town."

"Thanks for the tip."

"No problem, thanks for bringing in the books. I'll have some students set them up."

"I'm sure Mike would be more than willing to help set up ours."

"We can always use the help." Joey said and lowered the handicap access lift. "Mike, just give a yell, when you have every thing on the lift."

"Why'd you go and say that?" Mike asked.

"Because you're the fifth column." Brian said.

"Excuse me."

"Just remember to keep an eye out for number 17."

"Why?"

"All the books are labeled with the seller's number and price. That's how the DAF folks keep track of who sold what."

"So what."

"So 17 is selling quality destructualism."

"Okay."

"And don't buy anything with number 60 or 70."

"Because they're structuralism."

"No. Those are our numbers, the remainders from Daedalus and the DAF takes 20 percent off the top."

"And I'd be buying books we already own."

"And we'd lose money."
"So how do you want to work the sale?"
"After you set up our books, and make sure that's just before ten o'clock, make your way to the lounge."
"Where's that?"
"Up there. See how it kind of horseshoes around the staircase and the newel."
"You mean that thing in the middle of the staircase."
"Yep."
"Looks like a totem pole to me."
"It's a symbolic newel, they're anthropologists."
"So how am I supposed to I get in?"
"There's doors on both sides of the mezzanine."
"So I get to pick, before any one else gets in."
"That's the idea."
"I always wanted to be an inside man."
"Let's say you're getting a little head start, that's all."
"You want to help me load the lift?"
"I'm going back to the truck and get us some bags and a blanket to cover what we buy."
Mike put the loaded four stacks and two boxes on the platform. Brian returned with the bags.

"Here, you take half," Brian said, "I brought a dozen, we can always get more if we need to."

"Where are you going to be?" Mike asked.

"I'm going to go mingle with the dealers, see if I can get a better spot in the line."

"I mean during the sale."

"I think I'll work my way up the inside of the staircase. . . ."

"Around the totem pole."

". . . and then work down the outside."

"Around the newel."

"Right. Then we trade places, and I'll do the lounge."

"We should be done by noon."

"I doubt it. We'll keep repeating the process until they run out books, or we run out of time."

"Three o'clock. That's five hours of climbing stairs."

"The exercise will do you good."

"You're the one with the spare tire."

"I am a full-figured guy. I could go on a diet, I suppose. You, on the other hand, would need to take growth hormones."

"Touché."

"I'm going to go see if I can start a conversation with Romanowski."

Brian left and Mike went to find Joey.
"Say Joey, I could use a hand with your elevator."
"I'll be right there." Joey said.
"Take your time."
Joey walked over to Mike. "All you have to do is press this button." Joey said.
"Thanks for the lift." Mike said.
"My pleasure, believe me."
"So where do you want me to put the stuff."
"I wish you hadn't asked that question."
"Brian said you were saving us a space."
"Yes. Yes, indeed. Over there, on the right side."
"By the totem pole?"
"Exactly."
"You know that's not a bad location."
"Is it wrong?"
"No, it looks pretty good to me."
"Echo is a friend of the Family."
"Not mine, ask my mother."
"Very well then." Joey said and strolled off.
Mike unpacked the boxes and arranged the books in rows on the first flight of stairs. There were multiple copies of several titles. He split them up,

putting each copy on a different step. When he finished, he flattened the boxes and stopped to admire his work.

By ten minutes to ten, and the line outside was getting restless. Looking noticeably nonchalant, Mike moseyed over to the mezzanine. The books were arrayed on the floor in rows. Mike opened two of his bags and spotted a collection of Hegel titles. He glanced at the prices and thumbed through the first two. They weren't marked up so Mike put them all in the bag. He spotted four old hard-cover Margaret Mead titles. He picked up the first one, *Coming of Age in Samoa*, and looked at the price. It was marked down ten percent and badly marked up and underlined. Maybe some student would find that a bargain, but Ernie would kill him if he bought it. Mike put it down. Four boxes down, there were six Penguin Classics, Mike bagged them.

The doors downstairs opened. The dealers at the head of the line pushed through the doorway and started to run towards the books. Brian chugged along in the rear. The lounge filled with people. Three Loeb Classics caught his eye. Mike bent down to pick them up, when someone reached between his legs and grabbed the books. Mike stepped back and then tried to work his way back to the books. The crowd was two

and three deep. Mike tried to wedge himself between people so he could see the books.
 An hour later, Brian came into the lounge and nudged Mike.
 "So, you find anything?" Brian asked.
 "At least four bags. It's like shooting fish in a barrel." Mike said.
 "That's all?"
 "Yeah, well, some of the prices are weird, and a lot of them are highlighted or underlined."
 "Students. Forget the prices. Pick up anything good, we can dump the overpriced and marked-up stuff later."
 "Grab first and ask questions later."
 "Right. Bring your four bags and mine down to the first floor and cover them with my blanket. I'm going to see if I can find a Men's Room."
 Mike negotiated a path down the stairs and parked the seven bags next to the staircase.
 "Joey, okay if we leave these here, while we look around some more?"
 "Hey, like it's not a problem, you know, I'll just mark them sold, that's all."
 "Don't bother, I'll just cover them with Brian's blanket."
 "Whatever you want to do is fine with me."

Mike covered bags with the blanket and headed back upstairs. The rows of books were beginning to thin out and people were stepping into the empty spaces. Brian wasn't in the lounge, Mike finally found him on the landing between the second and third floor.

"So, you find a john?" Mike asked.

"Yep, unfortunately. There's one on three, between the seminar room and the classrooms or offices or whatever." Brian said.

"Good to know."

"Ah, Mike, I wouldn't recommend using that one, if I were you."

"Hey, I don't care if it smells."

"I think there were a couple of gay blades in the stall, if you know what I mean."

"Any holes in the side of the stall, you know, by the urinal?"

"Nope. None that I saw."

"Then who cares. Live and let live, that's what I say."

"Let's switch. You take the stairs, I'll take the lounge."

"Be my guest."

Mike worked down the inside of the stair case. He picked up speed and more books. When he reached the second floor, his two bags were full, so he headed down to one and put them under the blanket. Back on the second floor, he found four hardcover volumes of Jung's Complete Works. He tried to remember if the hardcover edition was out of print and decided it didn't matter. He put the books under his arm. He spotted a row of Dover books, put down the Jung, and added the Dover books to the stack. He braced the top with his chin, reached under the stack and carefully walked to the to the first floor. Brian was putting a bag under the blanket.

"I told you nothing with 60 or 70 on it," Brain said, examining Mike's last bag.

"You told me not to look at the label." Mike said.

"I told you not to look at the price."

"Right. So I just picked the kind of books we sell."

"Those are ours. I priced them yesterday."

"I thought they looked familiar."

"I'm going to get some more bags."

"Get some for me too."

"You want a sandwich?"

"Nah, we're not going to be here much longer."

"Mozzarella and onion on whole wheat pita bread."

"I'm not that hungry."

"I got ketchup too."

"I think I'll check out the outer perimeter of the newel."

"Suit yourself, I'm hungry."

"Somehow I'm not surprised."

Brian went to the truck. Mike decided to look for Nancy. She usually went to the DAF book sale and she had no way of knowing he was working there. He would surprise her. He passed the check-out and Romanowski gave him the thumbs up. Mike waved back. One-thirty and the dealers were leaving, Mike made a note to mention it to Brian. He climbed the stairs to the mezzanine and then circled the lounge. No sign of Nancy. He walked up the rest of the staircase. On the landing between two and three, he spotted Magda. He looked around and saw no sign of Petr or Nancy. Mike gave up and started to look for books. On two there were several issues of Glyph and Yale French Studies. He brought the load down to one. Sated, Brian approached Mike and handed him six bags.

"You're lucky that Ernie likes journals, most dealers don't." Brian said.

"That's probably why they were still there." Mike said.

"Otherwise, this is looking good."

"Yeah. Romanowski gave me the thumbs up as he was leaving."

"Yep, I talked to him outside. He said he was going to a library sale in Arlington Heights."

"So maybe it's time to go?"

"Nope, the dealers may have other sales to go to or they don't know that Joey keeps putting books out until almost three."

"We could just wrap it up, you know."

"Think of it this way, with the dealers gone, it'll be a whole lot less crowded."

"In case you'd like to know, I saw Magda between two and three."

"What is she doing here?"

"Buying books, but that's just my wild guess."

"Is Peter with her?"

"No sign of Pete or Nancy."

"Well, next time you see him, don't mention it."

"I got my own troubles."

"Fine. Just don't add to theirs."

"How about we look for books?"

"Nothing I would enjoy more."

"You want to work up or down."

"Down."

"I guess I'll work up then."

Mike and Brian returned to book hunting. An hour later, they met up, in the lounge.

"Find much?" Mike asked.

"Not much. But I did find four Margaret Mead first editions. Not only that, they're presentation copies to Malinowski and they are heavily annotated." Brian said.

"Wish I had seen them." Mike said.

"You sure you saw Magda Prst?"

"I know what she looks like."

"Well, I never ran into her."

"Me neither, I mean again, so she must have left."

"It's almost three, what do you say we wrap this one up?"

"I'd tie the ribbon."

They carried their bags down to the first floor and added them to the pile.

"Looks like a pretty long line to me." Mike said.

"Not as long as the line to the john." Brian said. "Let me see if we can't get Joey to check us out."

"Shouldn't be hard."

Brian wandered off and returned, five minutes later, with Joey in tow.

"Okay Mike, this is the way we decided to work it." Brian said. "I'm going to go through the books and hand them to Joey. He's going to add them up and the give them to you to box."

"Where'd you put our boxes?" Mike asked.

"Just grab some of those over there." Brian said, pointing to a pile of empty boxes. Mike retrieved ten boxes.

"They've got staples holding the bottom shut." Mike said.

"So what." Brian said.

"So how are we supposed to break them down for Ernie's stockpile?"

"We won't, we'll toss them."

"Isn't that ecologically incorrect?"

"Just pack the books."

"Okay, but you're the one that's going to have to answer to Kate."

Mike waited and wondered which of his picks Brian would reject. Brian looked through the first bag and passed it to Joey. Mike packed the books as Joey handed them to him.

Half an hour later, with six boxes full and no comments from Brian, Mike grinned to himself. He stacked those boxes near the wall and began another box. As he put the first five books in the seventh box, the stack toppled over with several low thuds and a low pitched boom. Mike jerked towards the commotion and hooked his thumb on a box staple.

"Ow! What was that?" Mike asked

"Your boxes fell over." Brian answered.

"And the bang?"

"Some other butterfingers dropped must have his box."

"Hey, it's not funny."

"Okay, maybe it was just an echo."

"I snagged my thumb on one of your staples. Look I'm bleeding." Mike said and held his thumb up for Brian to inspect.

"I'll get the first aid kit." Joey said.

"Hey, it's not that bad." Mike said.

"Before you pass out, Sleeping Beauty, why don't you wash it off and wrap a towel around it." Brian said.

"I'm calling a lawyer." Mike said.

"We don't want you damaging the merchandise, now do we."

"You're all heart."

"Joey, where's the closest men's room?" Brian asked.

"There's still a line for the toilet on the mezzanine. He would be better off using the one on the third floor."

"Thanks guys." Mike said and plodded up the stairs, sucking his thumb. He bumped into a woman coming down the stairs, mumbled "Excuse me", and turned to see if it was Nancy, but it was a blonde. He found the john on the three. At the sink, he carefully examined the wound in the mirror and watched blood roll down his thumb and drip to the floor. Then he turned on the cold water, rinsed his right thumb under cold water and wrapped it carefully in a paper towel. He moved left, to the urinal, and relieved himself. The guy in the stall to his left moaned and Mike decided it was time to leave.

"You okay?" Brian asked.

"I'm fine and I'm not the only one." Mike said.

"Zorros?"

"Yes, of course, the gay blades. Perhaps I should have warned you." Joey said.

"Any problems?" Brian asked.

"Nah. One of them seemed to be having a good time, that's all." Mike said

"That toilet does have a reputation. But then again, I ask you, is it wrong?" Joey said.

"Nah. Don't worry about it." Mike said.

"Well then, let's get back to work, maybe we'll be able to get out of here by four." Brian said.

"I'll straighten the boxes."

"Just watch your thumb. I don't want you getting blood on the books, it wouldn't be kosher."
"What's kosher got to do with books?"
"A staple is not a mohel."
"Moil?"
"It rhymes with O'Boyle."
"Right. Double trouble, moil and bubbles."
"Never mind. Let's get on with it."
Slowly they worked the last ten bags into the boxes.
"Thanks Joey, I think we had a pretty successful sale." Brian said.
"My pleasure, as always." Joey said.
"Do you want a check now, or do you want to take it out of our sales?"
"It would make bookkeeping a lot simpler, if you paid now."
"Fine. Mike you watch the stuff."
Brian disappeared with Joey to settle the Echo Books account. While Mike waited, police appeared at all the entrances to Haskell Hall. They dispersed through the crowd. One group seemed to like the books on three. Brian reappeared with a smile.
"With luck, what we sell will cover what we bought."
"What's with all the cops?" Mike asked.

"Chicago's finest? Probably looking for a shoplifter. Do you want me to ask Joey?"

"Nah, I was just curious."

"Let's load the van, the hand trucks are in the corner."

Mike untied the hand trucks and said, "I think I'll take four this time."

"I figured you might."

"Let's get these babies back to the store and call it Rooster time."

"Robert's sounds good to me."

They loaded two hand trucks and lowered them using the lift. A lean cop and a gaunt student were standing between the double doors of the back entrance, as they descended.

"That's him!" The student said, pointing to Mike.

"Hey Mike, I think he's pointing at you." Brian said.

"Must think I'm the shoplifter." Mike said.

The policeman walked toward Mike.

"Excuse me, sir, the Field Lieutenant wants to talk to you."

"Me?"

"Yes, you."

"Excuse me, Brian, my help is needed elsewhere." Mike said.

"I'll wait here." Brian said.

"I'll be right back. It shouldn't take long, after all, I didn't see the shoplifter."

"If you will just follow me."

Mike looked at the officer's name plate, "Sure, Officer Neruda, whatever you say."

"Sergeant Neruda. The Lieutenant is waiting for you in the reading room, up this way." Neruda said and led Mike to the lounge.

"What's his name?".

"Gruber."

They left the lounge and went down the corridor on the right to the reading room. The room was filled with chairs around a large L-shaped library table. At the head of the table, a stout policeman sorted some papers.

"Ah, excuse me, Lieutenant, we found the guy." Sgt. Neruda said.

"Excellent. Good job, Wayne. Let me know when the MCU gets here." Lt. Gruber said.

Sgt. Neruda left the room.

"Have a seat."

"Thanks, who's the MCU?" Mike asked.

"Mobile Crime Unit."

"Some sort of lab thing."

"So what did you say your name was?"
"Michael Rek. I didn't catch your name either."
"Gruber, Vic Gruber."
"If it's okay with you, I'd just as soon call you by your last name?"
"Only my family calls me Victor."
"All right then."
"Well, Mike, what were you doing in the third floor men's room at three o'clock?"
"I took a leak."
"What's wrong with your thumb?"
"I caught it on a staple from some stupid box."
"Did you have a homosexual encounter?"
"Hey, I'm engaged. I'm just here for the book sale. I work for Echo Books over on 53rd."
"So while you were allegedly urinating, did you notice anything unusual?"
"Some guy, in the stall, he groaned."
"Your friend?"
"Nah, I was running my thumb under some cold water."
"I thought you were urinating?"
"That's right, sorry, first I rinsed my thumb and then I took a leak. Honest."
"Probably the lungs collapsing."
"My lungs are fine, it's just my thumb."

Sgt. Neruda came back into the room. "Lieutenant, the MCU is here."

"Good. Take this witness over to Wentworth. Take his statement. You know, the usual." Gruber said.

Chapter 4

Sgt. Neruda dropped Mike off at Robert's Roost, just in time for the kickoff of Monday night football. Exhausted, he sunk on a stool next to Brian. Brian was talking to the professors again.

"Hi Mike, I was just telling George and John about the suicide over at the book sale." Brian said.

"A suicide, huh, the cops never mentioned it to me." Mike said.

"Well, that's what the rumor is."

"Probably some depressed grad student, it usually is, thought he failed his prelims." George suggested.

"Maybe a book dealer? Disheartened by all the books that Brian purchased." John countered.

"I doubt it," Brian said, "we didn't get that much, maybe ten boxes."

"Yeah, something like that." Mike agreed.

"Ten boxes sounds like a lot to me. So, Mike, Brian was telling us how you were assisting in the investigation. Any major breakthroughs you would care to share with us?" John asked.

"It was stupid. A waste of four lousy hours. They just had me tell over and over again how I took a leak." Mike answered.

"Yes, I suppose there can't be that many ways one can take a leak."

"Yeah, right. And one cop kept hinting that I was there to meet my lover."

"Mike, I didn't know. I want you to know that just because you're queer doesn't mean I won't talk to you. Heck, many of my better friends have been queer." George said.

"If I ever decide I'm gay, you'll be the first to know." Mike said.

"Ahem, George, don't you think this queer thing is a tad not PC, departmentwise?" John said.

"Politically correct? Nobody in our department would dare call someone, who is one-third African American, one-third Cree and one-third Polish, politically incorrect." George said.

"How can you be three different things like that?" Mike whispered to Brian.

"I don't know, but knowing George, I wouldn't ask him. It's just those one of things, either he's telling the truth and it's a long story, or he's making it up and it will be an even longer story." Brian said.

"He looks Hispanic to me?" Mike said.

"My mother was D.A.R." George said.

"Your mother's dead? You have my sympathies." Mike said.

"Daughters of the American Revolution."

"You really haven't told us any more than Brian already has." John said to Mike.

"Hey, you asked. I didn't say I knew anything. I spent the last four hours answering questions and sitting around. Brian at least had time to ask some questions."

"Yes, well, Brian perhaps you should inform young Mike of the developments in the case so far." John said.

"Sure John. There's not a whole lot. From what I've been able to make out, some student entered the men's room just as you were leaving. I guess he was waiting for the stall, anyway he hung around for a while." Brian said.

"Probably one of my queer friends." Mike said.

"And then he got impatient or mother nature did, so he decided to see if there was actually anybody in the stall or if the door was just stuck. The door was locked, but he spots this foot at kind of a weird angle under the door. So he peeks over the top and sees blood. He calls the police."

"That's the guy that was pointing at me?"

"Yep. I think so."

"No wonder."

"George, it's getting close to nine, you want a ride?" Brian asked.

"No."

"I thought you had to be home by nine, or your wife wouldn't serve you dinner?"

"Ten, and it's football season, so I get Monday nights off as well as Sundays. She's down at the Cove, watching the game with her girlfriends. I'll get a pizza to go from Robin, Mary won't be home until late." George explained.

"Well, do what you want, it's past my bedtime." Brian stood up and nodded at the three of them and then turned to Mike. "You want a ride?"

"Sorry, but I think I'll stay at Nancy's tonight, it's been a long day." Mike said.

"Whatever. See you tomorrow."

"Later."

Mike surveyed the bar for Nancy. She was sitting with the Peggys, enrapt in some sort of conversation. Turning back to the bar, Mike asked, "So what's your specialty? What do you guys teach?"

"Well, my dissertation, is in early English literature, but these days, so much of my time is taken up by divisional responsibilities that I barely have time to teach my Beowolf class. George, on the other hand, still has his two famous classes." John said.

"What do you mean by that?" George asked.

"Two of the most popular courses in the department are George's Revolutionary Literature, and his Postmodern Poetry. Both big hits with the students."

"I haven't had a real student since I gave up the Contemporary Poetry class."

"Remember George, I have already explained that to you. We brought in Katya Clovek to cover feminist interpretation, in order to answer the needs of the women."

"It was my course."

"Look, you handle your courses, let Katy handle hers." "So I have to teach two courses, just because she shows up?"

"Face it George, you are never going to be a feminist."

"I understand all oppressed peoples."

"Well, why not be revolutionary and teach Revolutionary Postmodern Poetry and Prose?"

"You'll back me on this?"

"Of course. I'll have to ask around, of course. The usual hand-holding, that's all. Of course, we will have to find a lecture hall, maybe Harper 130."

"You know I only teach discussion classes, why put me in a lecture hall?"

"Ah, excuse me, but my fiancée is ordering some drinks, I think I'd better talk to her." Mike interrupted.

"You have never understood Postmodern Poetry have you. Admit it." George said.

"Later, folks." Mike got up from his stool and walked toward Nancy who had ordered a round and was chatting with Bonney. Looking aside, Bonney caught sight of Mike and gestured to Nancy. Nancy stood and placed her hands on her hips. Mike placed his hand on her shoulder.

"Boy, am I glad you're here. I've had a really rough day, can I stay at your place tonight?" Mike asked.

"What do you think you are doing?" Nancy said.

"Huh?"

"Kaz asked me what was going on with me and Zoltan."

"Why?"

"He said to ask you."

"Beats me."

"I've never heard of anything so juvenile in my life. How dare you?"

"All I said was, my woman has gone dancing with another man. That's all. I can't help that Kaz took it the wrong way."

"That's right, we never discussed whether ours was an open or closed relationship, did we?"

"I always thought, you know . . . ."

"You always think you think."

"I take it I'm not staying at your place tonight."

"No."

"Maybe tomorrow?"

"Maybe next week, maybe next month. I don't know, I think I need a break from you, maybe next year."

"I see," Mike turned and looked at the bar, "Well, have a good time."

"Good Night, Michael."

"'Night."

Mike stared at the bar and didn't want to look up. Bonney waited a few minutes. Pretending to wash some glasses, she watched Mike out of the corner of her eye. A sad, knowing sympathy dropped over her eyes.

"Hey, Mike, can I get you a beer or something?" Bonney asked.

"An Old Style'd be okay."

Bonney uncapped the beer and placed it in front of Mike. Mike reached into his pocket for money.

"Don't worry about it, this one's on me." Bonney said.

"Thanks."

"And don't worry about Nancy, she's just pissed off, that's all. Just give her some time."

"I don't know. Just seems like I got up on the wrong side of the world today."

"Rough day."

"Yeah."

"Well, if you want my advice, don't try to share your misery with Nancy tonight."

"I figured that."

"Just be careful. Maybe it's just this woman's perception, but you two seem to be drifting apart. I don't know, I kind of like you guys, I just hope you two can stay together."

"What do you mean? We get along fine, probably get married some day. It's just one of those days."

"Like I said, maybe it's just my perception."

"Like you girls know everything."

"Well, if you think you've got it rough, check out the tall blonde that just walked in with Professor Tuzeman."

Mike turned to see Bela Tuzeman gently lead a pale, hunched woman to the Peggys' table. Her reddened eyes scanned the table and looked back to Tuzeman. He smiled, nodded and introduced her to the table. Mike strained to hear what he said.

"She's not that tall." Mike said.

"She's no Thumbelina, if you ask me. If she just straightened herself out, you'd see how tall she is." Bonney said.

"You're all heart."

"I can be."

"So who do you think she is?"

"How would I know? I've never seen her in here before."

"Well, with Nancy at the table, I'm sure I'll never know."

"I'll let you know, if I hear anything."

"You're right though, she looks like she's had a rougher day than me."

"By a long shot."

"How old do you think she is?"

"I don't know, maybe forty. Hard to say, I don't know whether she always looks so haggard."

Petr walked in and sat down, a bar stool down from Mike.

"Haggard?"

"You know, worn out, exhausted, that sort of thing."

"I know what it means. I'm just surprised you used it."

"I went to college too, you know."

"Ah, Bonney, I think you have a customer," Mike said and gestured to Petr.

"Pete can I get you something?"

"Heinekens, if would be so kind." Petr said.

"Sure, no problem." Bonney replied.

"Hey, Mike, how goes it with you?" Petr asked.

"Long day." Mike said.

"Long day. Boy, let me tell you."

"What happened to your face?"

"All day long everyone ask me. You get in fight? You mugged? What happen to you?"

"So what did you say?"

"I fall down stairs."

"Wow, nothing is safe these days."

"I no think they believe me."

"You know how people are."

"Maybe, I not tell nobody nothing."

"Who cares what they think."

"I no care."

"That looks like a pretty wicked fall. Your eye's all swollen and that's a nasty gash on your forehead."

"I have hard head. You know those Czechs, they put me in prison. Czechs. Well, I no tell those

Communists nothing. Beat me up, Czech, I tell you nothing."
"You were in prison?"
"In the old country, that why I leave."
"How did you get out of prison?"
"Dubcek, of course."
"Who's he?"
"For once, the Czechs make big mistake, make Slovak Prime Minister."
"That 'Prague Spring' stuff? I think my folks talked about it. It's hard to remember, I was only four at the time."
"It was something, believe me. I was lucky, I escape, my brother send for me, sign papers."
"Why?"
"Because Czechs call Soviets, get rid of Dubcek. I lucky man."
"So you escaped with your wife?"
"No, I meet her in States. My sister-in-law introduce."
"I always thought you had met her in the old country."
"You want to hear how I escape?"
"Ah, not tonight, maybe some other time."
"It good story."

"I thought the Slovaks had some sort of trouble with the Hungarians"

"Now that we be small country, only five millions, the Hungarians get ideas. They have ten millions, they act like Czech."

"I heard a rumor that your wife was Hungarian."

"No, she born in Kosice. I born there too."

"Maybe, you're really Hungarian."

"If I Hungarian, then you Czech."

"So, who do you have in the game tonight."

"Buffalo."

"I got the Bills too. I wish I hadn't picked the Packers to beat the Bears."

"You should never bet against Bears. It is your team, home team."

"I hate the Bears. When I pick them to win, they lose. When I pick them to lose, they win. I can't figure it."

"Be sure to tell me team you pick next week, maybe I take Bears low."

"Do you think the Jets have a chance in this one."

"Homefield."

"There's that."

"Maybe they have chance, not tonight, maybe the other way."

"You mean at Buffalo?"

"Yes, at opponent's field."

"If they can't win at home, how can they . . . "

"It no sport, you American think gambling is sport, not like real football, what you call soccer. When the national team beat U.S.S.R., that is sport."

"If you don't like it, why bother entering in the pool?"

"My brother, he tell me, you are in America now, you must be like American. So, I play in football game."

"Right, The Melting Pot."

"What you say?"

"Nothing. I was just thinking about a book, by a guy named Handlin."

"Don't tell me how to handle. You drunk."

"Sure, I've had a couple."

"You talk nonsense."

"Nonsense?"

"I am American citizen now. Why not you talk to you're buddy, Mister Policeman."

"What? Oh, Tony's here, thanks Peter."

"It's big trouble, policeman."

"Don't worry, Tony is okay. He comes here all the time."

"Policeman put you in prison."

"I've never done anything, why would he arrest me, come on Peter."

"Because they are bullies. They will find way."

"Doesn't sound like Tony to me."

"You are still young man, I see."

"I'm not that young, I'm 28."

"Okay, 28, be sure you pay rent on Sunday, or I show that you are foolish young man."

"Excuse me, Pete." Mike said and turned to Tony. "Hey, Grata, I went by where you work today and there was no sign of you."

"Yeah, Neruda mentioned it. Thanks for telling everybody how I was your good friend." Tony said

"I figured it couldn't hurt, let them know I know a cop."

"Mike, I'm not your average cop. Next time, don't do me any favors, okay?"

"Sure, whatever you say, sorry if I caused any problems."

"Oh, I can handle Neruda. It's just that I like to have some warning when I have to."

"Okay."

"So you met the 'Bulldog'?"

"That lieutenant guy?"

"Field Lieutenant Victor Gruber."

"Yeah, he was okay. You think he's gay?"

"Gruber? No way."

"He asked me if I was having a homosexual encounter, whatever that means. I figured it might be some sort of come on or something."

"He's been married as long as I've known him."

"So. These days, you never know."

"Plain old-fashioned married."

"Well, some of your buddies at the station are."

"Sure, my guess would be about ten-percent. I take it that came up again at the station."

"Yeah, one cop seemed convinced that I was in the john to meet my lover. Couldn't believe that I was there to take a leak and run my thumb under some cold water."

"During the interrogation?"

"They were taking my statement."

"Right."

"A guy can't even take a leak anymore. Whatever happened to 'Life, liberty and the pursuit of happiness', I should call the A.C.L.U."

"Take it easy."

"Why should I?"

"Gruber thinks it was a suicide."

"So."

"So they were just sweating you, that's all, you know, to see if you'd break down under pressure."

"I spent fours hours over there for no reason."

"Standard procedure, it's what I'd do, sweat the last known witness, see if you get anything."

"It's harassment of a taxpaying citizen. Maybe it's sexual harassment. Yeah, that's it. I should get a lawyer."

"You'd be wasting your time and your money. Besides you can't afford a lawyer."

"What if I offered him a percentage?"

"No lawyer would take the case for a contingent fee."

"Why not."

"Because you don't stand a chance of winning."

"Great."

Tony looked up at the television and started to follow the football game. Mike looked at his beer.

"You see, I was right. Bullies. Only bully make you go to prison for four hour." Petr whispered hoarsely.

"Not so loud Pete," Mike whispered and discreetly nodded toward Tony.

"Hey, I no care, they know who they are. Is your friend, not mine, buddy."

"Ah, right, shouldn't you be going home or something?"

"I go home as I please. Magda, she wait. I have my time, she have hers. When I drinks, I drinks."

"I know what you mean. I'm drinking with you guys, I'm drinking. Nancy will just have to wait until I'm ready to go."

"Man must be man."

"Sounds good to me."

"I go now. See what wife make for supper. I feel hungry just now."

"You sure you don't want another Heineken?"

"No, I must go."

"I'll, see you later then."

"Good-bye."

"'Night."

Petr got up, put on his jacket and walked to the door.

"I'd be careful around that guy, if I was you." Tony said.

"What, Pete? He's okay, he's just a janitor." Mike said.

"Maybe I see some things down at the station that you don't."

"Like what?"

"Like maybe, some of your drinking buddies have paid us some visits, which, perhaps, they choose not to mention to you."

"You're saying Peter is dangerous?"
"I'm not saying anything. All I said was, be careful."
"Okay, I'll be careful. I suppose you heard what he said?"
"I heard."
"Sorry."
"Happens all the time. What gets me is they're so polite to your face, but when they're talking to someone else and they know you can hear them, that's when you hear all the grief."
"That's passive resistance."
"Passive aggression."
"Right."
"So did you have Buffalo, tonight?"
"Yeah, but I was already out of it, I lost three games on Sunday."
"Lucky you, I think I lost five."
"Same difference."
"So who won?"
"I don't know, ask Andrew, I think it's Ken and Fergie, but I'm not sure."
"Ken's okay."
"Yeah, nice guy. Of course, I don't see him much."

"He's pretty much day shift, you should come in for lunch."

"Breakfast, I usually don't get up until maybe ten."

"Come in for breakfast then"

"Nah, breakfast in a bar would just be too weird for me."

"A lot of people do."

"I'm sure they do, probably start their day with a shot too."

"Say, remember that T-shirt Kaz used to wear?"

"Beer, it's not just for breakfast, anymore."

"That was a good one, makes me smile whenever I think about it."

"I wonder where he gets his T-shirts."

"I've got too many other more important things to worry about."

"Yeah, I guess we all do."

"These aren't the easiest of times."

"What do you think that student was worried about?"

"What student?"

"The suicide over at the University."

"What makes you think it was a student?"

"Hey, your buddies, sure didn't tell me nothing. Brian told me when I finally got here."

"Well, Brian's got it wrong."

"So if it wasn't a student, who was it."

"Sorry Mike, but I don't know if they've made an official statement yet. Technically, I'm not supposed to say anything to the public, until they do."

"Come on, it's not like I'm going to call some television station and report a hot news tip. I just want to know what kind of sorry individual ruined my day, that's all."

"I really shouldn't tell you this, but it was some big shot."

"A politician."

"No, a professor."

"I can't think of any big names in Anthro these days, except maybe Bela Tuzeman, and he's here."

"Did I say he was a professor here? No. Some kind of professor in town to give a speech, or something."

"Not Zoltan Gyula."

"Yeah, I think that was the guy's name."

"Wow."

"You knew the guy?"

"Nah. He was in here yesterday, that's all, and he's famous or at least his books sell."

"Some sort of international type?"

"I think he's Hungarian but teaches in Italy, some old university."

"Well, maybe that explains why the feds are all over the place."

"The FBI?"

"State Department, I think. Any time a famous foreign national is killed, they go into a tizzy, probably worried about an international incident or something."

"Even for a suicide?"

"They still get excited."

"Seems like a waste of time to me."

"They probably observed your interrogation at the station."

"I hope they learned how to take a leak or it was definitely a waste of taxpayer's money."

"Almost everything is, except cop's salaries of course."

"I suppose you'd have all the money go to the police?"

"Sure, why not? Actually I find the idea kind a nifty, when you put it that way."

"Wouldn't that mean martial law or a police state?"

"I guess it would be, certainly the press would call it that. Then again, maybe that would be another nuisance we wouldn't have to deal with."

"But what about the Constitution and all that."

"Look, we could have the muggers and the drug dealers off the street, like that. No more gangs. You don't think the average citizen, like yourself, would like that?"

"Didn't Jefferson say something like 'better that 99 guilty men go free, than one innocent man go to jail'."

"Yeah, well that's 99 perecnt of the bad guys out there. I'd rather take them all in. I could live with batting 990."

"But what about the one guy?"

"He probably did something we don't know about, I wouldn't cry for him."

"Pretty tough stuff."

"You should understand that I don't particularly approve of our form of government. But I'm not saying that it would ever happen."

"Well that's a relief. Otherwise, I might still be in jail, guilty of Gyula's suicide."

"Mike, the way it works now, only the bad guys walk. But I know you, I don't think you did anything. You figure it out."

Bonney came down the bar with a bounce and a smile. "You guys ready?"

"A couple Old Styles, this one's on me." Tony said.
"You ready Mike, or should I put it on ice." Bonney asked.
"Seems I'm always ready." Mike said.
"Just checking."
Bonney set two bottles in front of them, "So, I checked out the blonde, like you wanted me to."
"Which blonde is Mike after now?" Tony asked.
"None, I got Nancy." Mike said.
"The tall one at the table with the Marjorie, Rita and Gretchen." Bonney answered.
Tony looked over to the tables, "I saw her earlier, she looked like something put her through the wringer."
"Well, her name is Meg and her husband deserted her tonight."
"You got a chance buddy, the old rebound." Tony said.
"She's sitting with Nancy." Mike said.
"The husband. What a jerk. Came into Chicago without her, with their kid in the hospital. After their baby got out of the hospital, she came into town to see her husband, and he seems to be gone." Bonney said.
"Did you catch his name?" Tony asked.

"It was some foreign sounding name, Sultan Guru, I think." Bonney said.
"A rich playboy." Tony said.
"Zoltan Gyula?" Mike asked.
"Yeah, that's the guy's name."
"You know, he committed suicide today." Mike said.
"She has had a bad day."
"Now, that's what I call desertion." Tony added.

Chapter 5

"So who's today's special?" Mike asked as he entered the bookstore.

"Dylan Thomas, Sylvia Plath, Teddy Roosevelt, Paganini, and Fran Lebowitz." Brian said.

"That's not a special, it's a smorgasbord."

"Authors-of-the-Day."

"It's ridiculous."

"Ernie picks them."

"How am I supposed to remember five names?"

"Mike, use some mnemonic."

"Pneumonic?"

"Right, breath hard and think DTSPTRPFL"

"Dats Peter Pumpkinful."

"Never mind, I'm sure the customers will bring it up, should you miss it."

"To get the lousy 25% off."

"Why do you think they come in for the Author-of-the-Day."

"I always thought it was for a change of pace, Ernie's brilliant choice of authors."

"It's a promotion. Get them to buy something, they normally wouldn't buy." Brian said.

"Where does Ernie get these ideas?" Mike asked.

"Probably from his Prairie City days."

"I suppose he got the window ideas then too?"

"Probably."

"He must have had too much time on his hands. You know some times I think he tries too hard, and most times, I wish he hadn't."

"Bottom line, it's his store, his money. You want to do better, do it yourself."

"Maybe, someday, I'll even make that mistake"

"Knowing you."

"Why do you put up with it?"

"Maybe someday. Besides, I think he knows what he's doing. More than I can say for some of us."

"Well, I know one thing, I'm not going to any book sales with you anymore, not for a long while."

"Think of it as a change of pace."

"It put me through the paces all right."

"Too stimulating?"

"Too many changes these days."

"So why do you think Gyula did it?"

"Killed himself?"

"Yep."

"Isn't it supposed to be a cry for help or something."

"Maybe with attempted suicides, a little too late when they're successful."

"So what do you think?" Mike asked.

"Who knows, maybe he went back and reread his book, *Eros, Ecstasy, Death.*" Brian suggested.

"Yeah, if that wouldn't drive you nuts, nothing would."

"Actually, I'm half serious, maybe he got infatuated with death. You know, maybe he was studying and experimenting with the edge."

"Yeah, well that's one edge I'd stay away from."

"I think I read somewhere that Sylvia Plath did something like that. Wanted to see what the near death experience was all about. Tried suicide three times."

"She did kill herself, didn't she. Third times the charm, I guess."

"It's unclear, though. She had arranged to be discovered, but it didn't work."

"If that's true, then she was playing a pretty dangerous and stupid game."

"Who knows maybe it was just like you said, a cry for help."

Stealthily, Ernie snuck up behind them. "I know I pay you two to do something, but just what that is escapes me, at the moment. I do know that it is not to hold erudite conversations for your mutual entertainment." He said.

"Hi Ernie, Mike and I were just debating the merits of Sylvia Plath." Brian said.

"We were?" Mike asked.

"Of course. She's one of the Auteurs du Jour." Brian replied.

"As you both know, anything by or about Plath is a buy, besides that, save the conversation for the customers."

"Say, Ernie, why do you think he did it?" Mike asked.

"Who are you talking about and what has he done?"

"Zoltan committed suicide yesterday." Brian said.

"Well, well, I am sorry to hear that. A brilliant mind, Professor Gyula. Who can speculate what his troubles were? For myself, I have found that the mere possibility of suicide has gotten me through many a restless night." Ernie said.

"Now, that's a scary thought." Mike said.

"Not at all, it is comforting to know that there is always a way out. And discomforting to see my employees twiddling their thumbs."

"Don't worry, my thumb's sore, I'm not going to do any twiddling."

"Maybe you should have a doctor look at it?"

"Like there's health insurance here. If I go to a doctor, I couldn't afford to work here. You know what a doctor charges just to look into your room and say hello."

"Well, I am sorry, but you know how it is, we are just barely breaking even. There is no way we could afford those insurance rates. I'm sorry Michael, I truly am. If it were up to me, it would be a different world, but, unfortunately it is not."

"I hope I don't get gangrene."

"I do not hire people that get gangrene."

"I guess I'm safe then."

"One is never safe, especially if they own a bookstore."

"That's why you get those dreams."

"That is why, sometimes, I cannot sleep, what else would keep me up at night."

"Hey, I'm sorry, if I said anything."

"Mike, you cover the register. There are still about eight boxes left from the DAF sale that I want you to look up." Ernie ordered

"That's going to take some time."

"Well don't use Books In Print, use the CD-ROM, and have Kate finish whatever you cannot do."
"Sure, right."
"And Brian, why don't you go through Literature, pull out our sunset books and check for stale dates, say over a year or so."
"Does that include Pop Fiction or just straight Lit?" Brian asked.
"No, we pulled the genre fiction last month, just Literature." Ernie said.
"Do you want me to mark them down, if they're stale?"
"No, I want to look at them first, and see if there are any of those exceptions that break the rule."
"They're your rules."
"I guess they'll be my exceptions then."
"You're the boss."
"That I am. I have a house call over on Madison Park, I may not be back until late. I trust you guys can handle the store."
"Sure, no problem."
"In that case, I will get some book buy bags and I am on my way."
Ernie went to the back to get his book-buying gear.
"Boy, Ernie's not in a good mood." Brian said.

"Maybe you shouldn't have brought up Gyula." Mike said.

"How was I to know he slept with the idea."

"I thought you knew the guy."

"Ernie is kind of complex, he takes some getting used to."

"Yeah, well when you figure him out, let me know. Maybe we can call the complex: Bibliophiliamania Nervousa. Something scientific."

"I'd call it fear."

"Right, and I suppose some call it courage."

"A combination, you've got to have both to run a small business."

"Well, I better start looking up books or someone's going to get madder."

"I guess I'll start weeding Lit."

"Have fun, I know I will."

Using the PC, Mike first-priced a couple of boxes of books and dealt with maybe two dozen customers. At three-thirty, a school girl from St. Thomas walked in and asked, "Where would I find the Reader's Digest Condensed Books?"

Mike asked, "Is this for school?"

"No, it's for my mother's birthday. She has them all, except number 17." She said.

"That must be a rare one."

"Yes, that's why I want to get it for her birthday."

"Well, I'm sorry, I don't think we have number 17, but if we did, it would probably be on the bargain table," and Mike gestured to his left.

"How much?"

"Probably fifty cents."

"At Mister Powell's Bookstore I get them for free."

"Look, you find number 17, it's yours, okay?"

"Okay."

The girl went to look at the bargain table. Brian came up from Literature and asked, "Her again, I suppose she asked for number 17?"

"Yeah, it's her mother's birthday." Mike said.

"Who on earth would want to collect something as stupid as that."

"Hey, you could collect the whole set and probably pick it up cheap."

"But why?"

"Why collect anything."

A heavy set man with a ruddy complexion and smile approached the counter from the Humor Etc. section, and asked "Do you have Edward Crowley's *Notations on Skelton's Philip Sparrow?*"

"Brian, this sounds like a question that you'd be better at." Mike said.

"If we have it, which I kind of doubt, it would be in Literature." Brian said.

"In addition I would like, Milton's *Eulogies to Ben Johnson's Hat*." The customer said.

"Brian, that would be in Literature too, wouldn't it, either under Johnson or Milton." Mike offered.

"I suppose." Brian said.

"Since you're going back to that section, why not show this customer exactly where to look?"

"Sir, if you would follow me."

"Thank you, they were cited in the New Republic. I went to the Prairie City Bookshop, first of course, and they thought the books must be out of print, so I came here."

Brian led the customer to the Literature section. Mike tried to keep an eye on them, but Fergusson Lewis walked in and headed straight to the Paranormal Studies section. Mike's gaze flitted between Brian, the cash register and Fergie. Brian returned to the register, and said "I can't work in the aisle with that guy there. He keeps asking for obscure titles."

"I thought he was one of the Hyde Park weirdos." Mike said.

"He's just what Reid called the 'lost and lonely', he wants someone to talk to, that's all." Brian said.
"I'd probably have told him to get lost." Mike said.
"Don't take it so personally. Remember, the customers are dealing you as an anonymous servant."
"Their servant."
"Yep, they're not talking to 'Michael Rek', they're talking to 'bookstore clerk'."
"Here he comes again. Your master."
"Excuse me, where would I find John Updike's *Penis*?" The man asked.
"Probably on Mr. Updike." Mike answered.
"The impudence."
"I'm sorry, I've never heard of that title, are you sure it has been published?" Brian said.
"Of course. It was cited in the New Republic."
"Must be a new book, maybe it hasn't released yet."
"Imbecile. Let me speak to the manager."
"Brian is the manager." Mike said.
"The owner then."
"He's gone for the day." Mike said.
"What is his name?"
"Ernest Buchannon." Brian said.

"Mister Buchannon will hear from me," he said as he stomped his foot, turned and marched out the door.

"I'll bet he talks to Ernie." Mike said.

"Ernie knows the type, they miss the old booksellers. There used to be a bunch of curmudgeons that would have relished talking to that guy." Brian said.

"Like Woody Beach at Prairie City?"

"No, I was thinking more like Reid Michener, the 'Abominable' Schneeman, and of course Mr. Clark."

"Before my time, I guess."

"Those were the days when booksellers were grouches and the customers seemed to like it."

"Unlike today."

"These days, all we can do is to try to humor the old timers."

"I guess nostalgia isn't what it used to be."

"De-ja vu."

"All over again."

"Never mind."

"By the way I saw Fergie come in."

"What's he on today?"

"He didn't say anything."

"What did he look like?"

"He looked preoccupied."

"Probably cocaine."

"Why don't you go back to Lit, you can keep an eye on him from there. From here I can only see the top of his watch cap, up over the shelves."

"I guess I'd better get started, we don't need to give Ernie any more excuses to get mad, when that guy talks to him."

Mike was about halfway through the boxes when Fergie approached the front desk.

"Okay, if I use your phone, it's an emergency." Fergie asked.

"Yeah, sure, but no long distance." Mike said.

"Don't worry, it's cool."

Mike tried to listen to the number of times Fergie dialed on the rotary phone, but a line of customers had formed at the register. Fergie was definitely animated, but Mike couldn't make out what he was talking about, as Mike dealt with the line of customers.

A young college student asked, "Do you have *A River Runs Through Madison County*?"

"I don't know, but if we did, it would be in Literature. It's alphabetical by author."

"I can't remember who wrote it."

"Hey Brian, who wrote *A River Runs Through Madison County?*" Mike shouted at the literature section.

"Norman Waller." Brian shouted back.
"Check in the W's."
"Thanks."
"No problem."

Finally the line eased up and Mike eased back into his chair, his left ear cocked.

"Hey, man, don't worry . . . no . . . I ain't going to commit suicide . . . that's against the law . . . I don't want to spend the rest of my life in jail . . . no I'm not playing tonight . . . of course . . . good-bye." Fergie hung up the phone and turned to Mike, "Thanks for letting me use the phone."

"No problem. Talking to your mother?" Mike asked.

"Talking to God. We usually play chess on Tuesdays."

"Over the phone?"
"How else?"
"Well, you can't use our telephone for a game."
"Of course not. Ever since he lost our first game, the Big Guy won't play over the telephone, if he thinks that there is even a remote chance that the calls might be traceable."

"How does he feel about suicide?"
"Oh, he's definitely against it."
"Why?"
"I didn't ask. Remind me to. Well, thanks again for the phone, I've got to get going, something to do."
"Later."
Mike went back to the books. At four-thirty, he finished first-pricing the last of the DAF books. Addressing the literature section he said in a loud voice, "Hey Brian, I'm done."
Brian came out of the literature aisle, "I'm about done too, why don't you take your boxes to the back room, I'll watch the register. When you're done, I'll take my stuff back."
"Okay with me." Mike said.
Mike got the hand truck from the back room and carted the boxes to the spot where Ernie liked them, just to the left of his desk. After two trips, he brought the empty hand truck up front. "Your turn."
"I think I'll use the book cart, the books are just loose, I don't want to box them " Brian said
"I was just trying to do you a favor," Mike said and returned the hand truck to the back room. When he returned, Brian put three stacks of stale books on the cart and put them in the back room.

"Well, Ernie has his work cut out for him tomorrow, maybe he'll be too busy to deal with our friend," Brian said, when he returned.
"I doubt it, he always wants to talk to customers, part of his good service thing."
"Don't whine to me about that again."
"I'm just saying he's going to talk to the jerk."
"And don't call him a jerk around Ernie."
"Okay, okay. By the way, I don't think Fergie was on cocaine."
"What then?"
"I don't know, but he was playing chess with God."
"In here? Mike you should have called me over, that's a game I would love to see."
"Well, actually, Fergie called him to say he couldn't play tonight, something came up."
"Called him?"
"Yeah, they play over the phone."
"Yep, definitely not cocaine."
"Whatever it is I want to try it some time, under supervision of course."
"I'd be careful with something that let's you talk to God."
"People do it every day."
"They don't play chess him."

"You've got a point."

"Some things are just better left for others to explore."

"Like the dear and departed Gyula."

"Like Zoltan."

"In that case, maybe I will leave it to Fergie."

"Well, I'm going to head over to Robert's. Can you handle the store until Kate comes in?"

"Yeah. She's late again. I can handle it, even if she doesn't."

"Well, then I'm off to Chez Robert."

"The Roost?"

"Yep, catch up on the latest Hyde Park gossip, maybe just the latest Robert's gossip."

"I'll probably see you later then."

"Momentarily, unless I see you first."

"Right. Boy that sure is funny."

"Sorry, I couldn't resist. But seriously, I've got to get out of there buy nine, ten the latest."

"Whatever."

"See you later."

"Later."

Mike looked up that day's buys on the C-D, and then walked over to Philosophy and Western Theology and found a copy of *Eros, Ecstasy, Death* and settled in at the register. At six, Kate slumped into the store.

"You're late." Mike said.

"It's just so terrible, he was so happy on Sunday, why, why would he? We danced, we all danced, laughed and laughed. Why?" Kate said sadly.

"Maybe he finally decided to do it, and so, you know, he was finally at peace with himself."

"Maybe no mind can handle so many brilliant revolutionary ideas. The tensions, the contradictions, the hair-splitting uncertainty, any mind would explode."

"Implode first, would be my guess."

"Poor, beautiful man. He gave his life for humanity."

"Humanity?"

"Even you."

"Me?"

"Not so much that you sell his book, but think of all the other books that will be written about destructuralism."

"Yeah, the stuff never seems to end."

"There is a reason for that."

"Students, they're forced to read whatever is assigned, and then regurgitate it for their professor."

"You were a student once."

"Six years ago, and I gave them back everything they gave me."

"So you didn't learn anything?"

"I learned to play the game. Think like the boss. Do what the boss wants."

"I suppose that's part of it, but didn't you read Hegel, Lacan, Irigaray, Barthes, Nietzsche, Foucault, Gyula or Derrida?"

"Just enough to get through."

"And it didn't affect you, didn't make you look at the world differently?"

"Can't say that it did."

"What about James Joyce?"

"I could never figure out what a moo-cow was."

"That's just childlike."

"Childish maybe, but what do I care what it's like to grow up in an Irish boarding school. I'm not Irish or even Catholic."

"Universal truths?"

"Okay, you're Irish, do think Gyula committed a sin?"

"I'm not a practicing Catholic, but it was a sin."

"What kind of sin?"

"I don't know, mortal probably."

"Joyce would know."

"Well, with mortal sins you're soul is in jeopardy, unless you go to confession and repent."

"How can you repent, if you kill yourself?"

"Maybe it's a cardinal sin."

"What's a cardinal sin?"

"I'm not sure, I think the cardinal virtues are something like temperance, fortitude, prudence and justice, not your strong points."

"Thanks."

"Then again, maybe they're charity, hope and faith, I get them confused."

"I'd bet those aren't my strong points, either."

"Not."

"So what's a cardinal sin? Maybe, if you break one of the ten amendments."

"Ten Commandments. I don't know, God's forgiveness is infinite."

"He would have to get angry with blasphemy."

"She. Infinite is infinite."

"So Gyula could be forgiven?"

"I guess."

"Next time Andrew Greeley comes in, remind me to ask him what he meant by naming that book *Cardinal Sins*."

"You'll probably learn more than you want to know, certainly less than you need."

"Actually, I'm more interested in the seven deadly sins."

"I think the venial sins are more your style."

"Nah, venal sins that sounds like an Ernie thing, I'll stick with the heavies."

"I don't know if I remember them, I'm not sure that they're really church stuff, they might just be literary."

"Well, what are they?"

"Maybe covetousness, avarice, sloth, envy, anger, gluttony, lust, greed and pride."

"The Seven Deadly Sins?"

"Pride is the worst, I think, the sin of angels or something."

"Pride?"

"If you're proud, you think you have everything coming to you, it leads to all the others."

"I think I'll stick with imprudent and intemperate."

"Going against cardinal virtues."

"Think of it as batting 500."

"It's between you and Her, but I wouldn't make light of faith."

"I thought you didn't believe in that stuff."

"I'm not practicing, mostly because of abortion and birth control, but that doesn't mean that I don't have faith."

"Maybe She would reserve judgment, if I got it half right?"

"I don't know, I've got to get to work, I'm late already, ask Ernie he knows everything."

"Right, let's get to work. You planning to go to Robert's tonight?"

"I don't know when I can go back there, Professor Gyula was such a nice man, I'll always remember that I met him there."

"I guess I'll go alone."

"Your imprudent intemperance is going to kill you."

"There's a difference between self-destructive and suicidal."

"Time."

"Yeah, well, in that case, then the only cause of death is conception."

Chapter 6

"Say John, what would you call a sin?" Mike asked as he sat down next to Brian and the Professors.
"In which text?" John answered.
"Everyday life."
"Quite irrelevant. What tradition, which religious text."
"The Bible I guess."
"Which one: the RSV, NJB, NAB, REB, NRSV, BV, BHS or KJV?"
"That religious text that those Christians use."
"Oh that one, the JPB. In my book, the sins you should concern yourself with are the ones that cry to God for vengeance."
"Why?"
"Those are the are the ones where God will not wait for you go to hell, he comes right down and deals with them himself."
"Sounds like something I should know about."
"Let's see, Abel's blood cried out to him, so killing would be one, for sure. And I guess he heard a ruckus over Sodom and Gomorrah, so that got his attention."

"So murder and sodomy are out."

"I didn't say that, I was merely citing a literary text. What do you want? I'm certainly not God."

"And you certainly didn't read far enough into the text. What about the passages in Exodus and James, huh?" George interjected.

"I'm sure you'll us about them, George." John said.

"That's right, in Exodus it says that out of their slavery they cried to God and God heard them."

"So slavery is a sin." Mike said.

"And in James, it says, the cries of the underpaid workers were heard by God." George said.

"Sounds to me like I'm safe on those two, but Ernie may in big trouble on that last one."

"What are we talking about any way?" Brian asked.

"Nothing, Kate thought Gyula committed a sin when he killed himself, I was just trying to figure out what she meant." Mike said.

"But he didn't kill himself." George said.

"Brian said the police thought it was a suicide." Mike said.

"I don't care what the cops thought, they didn't find a gun."

"No gun? Hard to shot yourself without a gun." Mike said.

"Exactly."

"Actually, it's quite feasible, or not altogether out of the realm of possibility, that somebody may have picked it up." John said.

"Sure." Mike said.

"Guns are quite expensive these days, if I had a need for a gun, which I don't, by the way, and I happened to have been there, I might have picked it up." John said.

"And sell it to Fergie I suppose." Mike said.

"For self-defense, perhaps." Brian suggested.

"No, you would have gone for a license, I can't see you with an unlicensed gun." George said.

"Okay, but somebody might have." John said.

"Maybe. But if they don't turn it in soon, they're going to get in big trouble." Mike said.

"So, I don't get it. Why kill Gyula? Why here? And why on the third floor of Haskell Hall?" Brian asked.

"Why kill him period?" George said.

"I believe, Tony, our local constable, he said the wound was small." John said.

"A mob hit." George said.

"The Mafia?" Mike asked.

"Everybody knows that the mob always uses a .22 caliber bullet. It's their signature for an execution."

"I can't see Gyula involved with the Mafia, what would they want from an anthropology professor?" Mike asked.

"Where was he from?" George asked.

"Hungary."

"I asked where was he from, not where was he born. Where did he teach?"

"University of Bologna."

"And where do you think Bologna is?"

"Italy, I guess."

"I rest my case." George said.

"Maybe it was an assassination, the KGB." Brian suggested.

"That is ridiculous, why would the Russians bother? They have their hands full with domestic problems." George said.

"They do say he was involved with the Greens in Hungary." John said.

"The French again?" Mike asked.

"I doubt they have nuclear test sites in Hungary." George said.

"I wouldn't put it past them." Mike said.

"Maybe he offended someone in the Hungarian government." Brian said.

"Kate said the Slovaks don't like him because of some dam on the Danube." Mike said.
"So maybe the Czech secret police assassinated him." Brian suggested.
"Nonsense," George said, "The Czechs don't have a secret police."
"Okay, the Slovaks then." Brian said.
"They don't have one either."
"And I suppose the Poles, Hungarians, Rumanians, and Bulgarians don't either." Brian said.
"Of course they do."
"So what gives?" Mike asked.
"Czechoslovakia doesn't officially separate until the first of the year, so I doubt they maintain two secret services."
"So what." Brian said.
"Besides, I find it hard to believe they could manage that kind of operation, even if they wanted to." George said.
"Why not?"
"They're too small, too disorganized, too incompetent to run an operation of that scale in the United States."
"They could hire somebody." Mike suggested.
"How are they going to find somebody? I can't imagine a white guy walking into -- what's the name of

that gang? -- El Ruhkin headquarters, and ordering a hit." George said.

"Okay, what about the Slovaks in Chicago?" Brian said.

"They're not going to work for the secret police."

"I was thinking of, maybe one of those neo-fascist groups that are on the rise again all over Eastern Europe."

"What fascist group?" Mike asked.

"I think I read somewhere that Hlinka Guards were making a comeback." Brian said.

"I don't know anything about them." George said.

"Every once in a while, my B.A. in History actually pays off."

"I guess you know more about it than I do, so what were these guards?"

"Let me think, I know we covered this in Boyer's Modern European History class."

"In the meantime, I'm going to get another beer." George raised his bottle and gestured to Kaz, "Kaz, can I have another Double X?"

"Dos Equis, you celebrating something?" Kaz asked.

"Merely a change of pace."

"Anybody else, while I'm down at this end?"
"Old style."
"Augsburger."
"Old Style."
"Old Style, Augsburger, Dos Equis, Old Style, I think I can handle that."
"Yes, do your best." John said.
"After, World War One, in the new Czechoslovak state, there was this priest who wanted an autonomous Slovakia. Founded the Slovak People's Party. Slovakia for the Slovaks." Brian started.
"The church again, there's not one spot in the Eastern Hemisphere that the Catholics haven't tried to ruin." George said.
"What about the Western?" Mike asked.
"No, he died." Brian said.
"So who started these guards you're talking about?" George asked.
"Tiso." Brian said.
"If you're pissed off, just say so." Mike said.
"Joseph Tiso." Brian said.
"Another Joseph " George said.
"Apparently, Hitler put a lot of pressure on the guy to make him declare independence, part of the pressure he put on the central government." Brian said.
"And he did?" George asked.

"Tiso, sure, what would you do?"

"I'd tell him to get his mustache and his buddies out of my face."

"Yep, and Poland fell pretty quick."

"I think I remember that, just before the Munich Agreement and peace in our time."

"Yep. They never had a chance."

"So who were the Hlinka Guards?"

"Hlinka had founded the Slovak People's Party but he died in 1938. Anyway, the new independent Slovakia created the Hlinka Guards, or the party did, patterned them after the German SS and SA and the Italian Black Shirts. Black uniforms and the fascist salute, and every thing, they really got into it."

"And the people didn't mind?"

"I don't know, I guess they liked the idea of independence, after a thousand years of being dominated by the Hungarians and the Czechs."

"And nobody protested?"

"Not until late in 1939, when Tiso ordered all men between six and sixty into the Hlinka. But by then it was probably too late anyway."

"Amazing." George said.

"Yep, not only that, they really went after the Jews, I mean 75 percent of the Jews were killed."

"They were Nazis." George said.

"I think Boyer called them a vassal state."

"It's still inexcusable."

"I think they just sort of fell into it, you know like they wanted more autonomy, and got more they more than they bargained for."

"There's still no excuse."

"Why didn't the Prague government just give them more autonomy?" John asked.

"Probably more concerned with the German minority, give in to one, and every minority would make demands."

"Sounds penny-wise and pound-foolish to me." George said.

"Look at what's going on over in Eastern Europe these days." Brian said.

"I guess. It's curious, I read somewhere, it must have been the New York Times, that something like that was going on there now." John said.

"Yep, they're going independent again, but so are all the ethnic groups, wasn't Slovenia one of the first to split from Yugoslavia? What a mess." Brian said.

"No, I mean that the polls show that the majority of Slovaks don't want a separate state, 65 percent, but two expedient politicians, I believe their names were Mechar and Claus, came up with some sort of back room deal." John said.

"Don't they have to have a vote or hold a referendum or something?" Mike said.

"They wouldn't get the necessary votes. I think they're going to try to get the Parliament to pass it, something like that, but it sounds like a done deal to me." John said.

"So it's kind of like 1938, it's going to hit them before they realize what happened." George said.

"Democracy, I just love it." Brian said.

"Yeah, you sure they weren't from Chicago?" Mike asked.

"Familiar as it may sound Mike, no." George said.

"So do you think, the Hlinka Guards are in Chicago?" Mike asked.

"From Brian's description, I don't see why not." George said.

"Mike, there are no Hlinkas in Hyde Park, I was repeating what I heard in that class, that's all." Brian said.

"I sure hope you're right."

"There are no more Hlinka's in Hyde Park than there are witches. You don't believe in witches, do you?"

"Only Twisted Sisters. Thanks Brian."

"No problem. I've got to go, anyway, it's way after nine."
"I wonder if Mary has my dinner ready yet." George said.
"That reminds me, we have our weekly departmental conference tomorrow at nine." John said.
"Well, I won't be there." George said.
"George, I don't think I have ever seen you on campus before noon." John said.
"Not if there is anything I can do about it."
"See you later Mike." Brian said.
"Later."
The three rose, put on their jackets and left. After a minute or two Bonney came down to the front end of the bar. "What did you say to them, to make them all leave?" She asked.
"I mentioned the possibility of Hlinkas in Hyde Park." Mike said.
"What's a Hlinka. Oh, never mind. Kaz is in the kitchen, would you mind moving down the bar, that way I won't have to be marching back and forth all night long."
"I like this end."
"I'll buy you a beer."
"Okay."
"Old style, okay?"

Mike nodded.

"There's a spot between Magda and Andrew, by the television."

Mike took his half-empty beer and walked down the bar. There were two empty bar stools. Taking the stool closer to Andrew, Mike asked, "Mind if I join you?"

"Be my guest, I'd much rather talk than watch anymore of this mindless nonsense that passes for television programming these days." Andrew said.

"So how's Prairie City Books these days?"

"Oh, the usual mushroom treatment."

"What's a mushroom treatment?"

"That's when you're left in the dark and they pile manure on you."

"Doesn't sound good."

"You get used to it, I guess."

"I didn't think Woody was that kind of guy."

"I suspect most bosses treat their employees and customers differently."

"Didn't Ernie work at Prairie City, before he opened Echo Books?"

"Yeah, he did mail orders before he left, since then I've been doing them.

"So what's Woody like to work with?"

"A typical bookseller, jack of all trades, and master of none."

"Ernie thinks he's a master bookseller."

"I have yet to see one that could come close to even a semi-professional salesperson."

"So why the mushroom treatment?"

"Oh that started, when Woody married Penny, Woody always ran a discount store, and now Penny wants to a full service store."

"So."

"So Penny wants me to get the books sent out the same day and Woody can't spare anyone to help out."

"What did you do before?"

"In the old days, the mail orders ran in cycles, I'd catch up on the backlog during the slow spells. Now Penny's angry because stuff doesn't go the same day that the customer ordered it, and Woody's angry because Penny's angry, and they both blame me."

"Happy loving couples."

"Yes, they can ruin anybody's day."

"Yeah, well I've had a rough day, make that three."

"Well, you deal with Woodrow and Penelope some time, and see how you feel."

"I'm serious, this week is not going my way."

"Trust me. If I can handle Woody and Penny, then you can handle Ernie and Brian."
"Oh, they're okay, more than anything else, it's Nancy."
"Yeah, I noticed she was sitting with the Peggys, these days."
"She thinks I'm spreading rumors about her or something."
"I heard the one about you two getting engaged."
"That's not what I said. Not that I would mind."
"Count your blessings, she's in her late twenties isn't she?"
"Yeah."
"Your lucky she didn't snag you, like Penny snagged Woody."
"How's that?"
"The old-fashioned way. Woody was fooling around with a staff member, which was a mistake right there if you ask me, and Penny got pregnant."
"Kids."
"Kid."
"I don't know about kids."
"See what I mean, count yourself lucky."
"I use protection."

"The failure rate on those is something like 15 percent, and besides as my father used to say 'Mama's baby, Papa's maybe'."

"That's pretty cynical."

"Well it's been a while since I had any success in that department, not since Marguerita, and that was years ago."

"What happened?"

"Oh, it turned out we only had three things in common. We both loved good food, we both loved her, and we both hated me."

"Not you're ideal match."

"Oh, it was, but only on those three issues."

"So is anyone happy?"

"Penny and Woody."

"Magda and Peter."

"Rumor has it that they fight."

"Fight?"

"Okay, what I hear is, that Sunday, Peter was following her around, and when he got home, he was pissed off."

"Drunk."

"Most definitely. Anyway, Magda felt threatened, so when Peter came after her, she hit him on the head with a broomstick."

"Ouch. That would explain the contusion."

"It broke the skin didn't it?"

"It looked like a pretty nasty scab."

"A contusion is just one of those fancy medical names for your plain old everyday bruise, that is all."

"So if it broke the skin, it's not a contusion."

"The bottom line is, she's here and he's not."

"He said he fell down the stairs."

"And you believe him?"

"He said nobody would."

"Maybe there's a reason for that."

Mike turned and surveyed the Peggys table, Magda and Nancy were talking, Mel was flirting with Meg. "Mel, I can't believe that guy, he's after Gyula's wife."

"His widow."

"Widow."

"I think Mel is one of those guys, you know like a vampire, if they don't get laid every night, they're afraid they're going to die."

"Still, respect for the dead, and like he has a chance."

"With his looks he always has a chance."

"I actually kind of liked his James Dean phase."

"But not the Kevin Costner."

"No, in his Kevin Costner phase, he went after Nancy."

"I can see where that would rub you the wrong way."

"I didn't like Gyula taking her dancing either."

"Now that's an interesting case, was it a suicide as the police seem to think, or was it some sort of diabolical murder, that's the question, certainly in my mind."

"George seemed to think it was some sort of Mafia hit."

"Of course, George would come up with some nonsense like that."

"Gyula is from Italy."

"Geniuses, like Zoltan for instance, believe me they're strange guys, fanatical about their subjects, driven by some weird internal force, who knows. And spoiled by their parents, teachers, and probably made fun of by their classmates"

"But he had everything."

"So what, one of those chess masters, early in this century, he was the undisputed champ of chess for thirty straight years, had everything, right?"

"Sounds good to me."

"Well, Mister Genius, he winds up at the end of his life, playing God on the phone, and he was giving God a pawn, that's the part I kind of like."

"At least God won."

"I'll have to check on that for you, but somehow I kind of doubt it."

"So you think he killed himself, couldn't put up with the pressures of being a genius."

"I don't know. They're different from you and me. Fawned on by everybody, it must go to their heads, and in that case they'd feel like they controlled the world or something. And in any case, any normal human being would want to kill them. So take your pick, was he mad or was it someone else?"

"I suspect it was those guards."

"Guards? Excuse me, but I have to micturate."

"Siphon the old Python?"

"As you used to say, point percy at the porcelain."

Andrew swiveled, and headed towards the bathroom. Bonney reached up, stretched and turned the dial on the television. The nightly news came on. Mike waggled his empty bottle at Bonney's back and it failed to get her attention. Nancy approached the bar and stood shoulder to shoulder with Mike.

"Hello." Nancy said.

"Hello."

"Bonney, I would like a gin and tonic." Nancy said.

"Sure, no problem."

"Thanks."

Bonney mixed the drink and placed it front of Nancy.

"Take it out of here," Mike said, pointing to his money on the bar, "and get me an Old Style."

"Thanks Mike, but I can take care of myself."

Bonney turned her attention to the television, "whenever you guys are ready, let me know. Say isn't that your bookstore?"

"Where?" Mike asked.

"On the TV."

"Yeah, can you turn it up?"

"Sure," Bonney said and stretched again.

"You should get a remote."

"Tell Robin that."

The sound came on.

"*As we reported at six o'clock, Cook County Medical Examiner Robert Thompson has issued a statement. Upon performing the autopsy, he has determined that the death of Professor Zoltan Gyula, yesterday on the campus of the University of Chicago, was not self-inflicted, as we reported earlier. What the police department had characterized yesterday as a probable suicide, now appears to have been murder.*"

The bar became silent as everyone followed the story. Meg Furie-Gyula cried.

"*In an exclusive, Channel 7 Eyewitness News has learned that the police have a suspect in the murder. They are holding the night manager of this Hyde Park bookstore for questioning. At this time his identity has not been released. Caesar Cortez, Eyewitness News. Back to you Mindy and Chad.*"
"But that's not true," Mike protested.
Nancy's face flushed and tears welled in her eyes. "You bastard!"
"But I'm here."
Nancy threw her drink in his face and hurried out of the bar. Mike squinted as the gin stung his eyes.

Chapter 7

"Captain James Cook, Ted Williams, Evelyn Waugh and Erasmus?" Mike said, as he entered Echo Books.
"For once, you read the sign before you came in." Brian said.
"But what kind of special is that?"
"Same as usual, Ernie usually goes with birthdays, unless he's trying to move some old stock, then he tries some other excuse."
"Okay, I can see Waugh and Captain Hook. But Erasmus and Ted Williams, they don't seem to go together."
"Of course they do. Use you're imagination."
"Okay Mr. Joyce, what's the obscure connection that some poor slob is going to have to figure out to get his Ph.D."
"Mike, if you can't see it, I'm not about to tell you."
"A mystery, then. Who cares?"
"Hey, I saw that story about you on the news last night."
"I saw it at the Roost."

"Ernie is not happy."

"Can't be angrier than Nancy, she threw her drink at me."

"Not in your face?"

"Yeah, in my face."

"You're lucky you're not blind."

"I guess I can thank the tonic for that."

"She has a temper, that's for sure."

"She sure does. But once the cops catch the killer, she should calm down. Then she'll have to realize that I had nothing to do with it."

"I don't know, if someone threw a drink in my face, I'd slug them. It would be war."

"I couldn't hit Nancy."

"You know her better than I do, but I'd still watch out for Ernie."

"Why?"

"Because, it makes the store look bad."

"But I didn't do anything."

"It doesn't matter, the public is going to think that Echo Books employs killers."

"Come on Brian, you were there."

"Hey sales aren't that good, a little bad publicity and who knows."

"But . . . ."

"Just lay low when Ernie's around, okay, he can't decide whether to sue you or Channel 7."
"He could sue them for libel."
"Slander."
"What's the difference."
"Slander is spoken, libel is printed."
"Lies are lies, either way."
"Who's that exclusive source anyway?"
"There's a guy I could hit."
"Or introduce to Nancy."
"Both."
"No idea?"
"I think Caesar Cortez made it up."
"Or got confused, they did talk to you on Monday."
"That was two days ago."
"Hey, he's a reporter, what do you expect. For a reporter, I'd say it's close enough, but hardly an exclusive."
"I should sue him."
"For what? Defamation of character."
"Loss of affection."
"Leave the suing to Ernie."
"I don't see what he's worried about."
"There's always some group that wants to protest something."

"Somehow I can't see the U of C, or the Department of Anthropology protesting. After all, he finished his speech."

"We might lose a lot of anthro students as customers."

"Who cares."

"Do you like you're job?"

"It pays the rent."

"Think about that."

"Well let's get to work then."

"You take the register. Ernie's in the back, doing some bookkeeping. I'll see what he wants me to do."

Brian turned and headed toward the office. Mike settled into the routine. He looked up the stack of new arrivals on the CD, so that Ernie could price them. There weren't that many. There were only two customers in the store that Mike could see, so he turned the radio to National Public Radio. Terri Gross was interviewing Stephanie Coontz. Mike figured the author was on one of those promotional tours for her new book *The Way We Never Were*. Terri was doing her usual interview. Mike fidgeted, looking for something to occupy his time. He decided to straighten the American History and Area Studies. He hoped to find Coontz's book or something else by her.

Bored, Mike was almost glad when Sylvester walked in with his porkpie hat, knapsack and cigar in his partially closed mouth. Maybe he would talk about something else besides mercenaries and Navy Seals.

"The nerve, . . . of those dang-blanged Russians." Sylvester cursed.

"What's up now?" Mike asked.

"What did they think they were doing?"

"What?"

"An assassination, . . . that's what, . . . and on the soil of the United States of America. I can't believe it!"

"You're talking about that professor that committed suicide."

"Yeah, on campus, but it wasn't no suicide."

"The police said they thought it was."

"The coroner said he was shot in the back of his head. Tell me, how many people shot themselves in the back of the head. That's nuts."

"Not many that I know."

"That's right. But ask the victims of the KGB!"

"KGB."

"A bullet to the back of his head."

"Doesn't the Mafia do that?"

"No, . . . they use a steel-jacketed .22."

"How do you know it wasn't a .357 magnum or something?"
"The radio said they found a .52 caliber slug on the floor."
".52 caliber sounds pretty big."
".25, excuse me."
"So what's the big deal about .25 caliber bullets"
"That's what those KGB assassins use to do their dirty work."
"Wasn't James Bond's Beretta a .25?"
"Not any more it isn't!"
"Sounded like a good gun to me."
"Are you kidding, . . . it almost cost Bond his life. It jammed on him, could have killed him right then and there. Now he uses a Walther PPK."
"What caliber is PPK?"
"It's no caliber. It's German. Police Pistol Kurt."
"Kurt?"
"Yeah kurt, you know, short."
"So you think he uses a .25?"
"Nah, the PPK would be 9mm short or your 7.65mm auto. They made only made a hundred of the 6.35mm. Course, he could always get Q to make one."
"6.35mm is the same as a .25?"
"Obviously."

"Do you think the KGB used a 6.35mm Beretta?"

"Why would the do that? They got their TOZ and TK. Not to mention all the guns that they make in Eastern Europe."

"So maybe they used something made in Czechoslovakia?"

"Sure. Kohout makes the Mars, Niva and PZK. Dusek makes the Duo, Ideal, Jaeger and Singer. There's the CZ Model 22, 36, 45 and Fox."

"Okay, okay, I get the idea."

A woman rolled a baby stroller into the store. Instead of a baby, she had three bags of books on the stroller.

"I'll talk to you later," Mike said to Sylvester. Mike turned to the woman. "Books to sell?" Mike asked.

"Yes, I have a couple bags, is Ernie around or a buyer?"

"I'm a buyer."

"Well, I moving to San Francisco, and I don't want to move these books with me."

"Lugged the books around that one too many times."

"And I'm not going to make that mistake again."

"Yeah, books get heavy. It usually takes a couple moves before people decide to sell their books."

"Well, I just decided to go through the books and sell anything I'm probably not going to read again."

"I did that once with my closet, pulled out all the clothes that I was never going to wear again."

"I hope you saved the most unusual, for a costume party or a special occasion."

"I don't think so. If you want to look around, this will probably only take but a few minutes."

"That's all right, I'll watch, I'm not buying any more books until I get to San Francisco."

"So why are you going to San Francisco?" Mike asked, as he started to sort the books.

"I'm going to clerk for a judge."

"You're a lawyer?"

"Graduated in June."

"You wouldn't know anything about libel suits would you?"

"Sorry, but they just teach us the theory, and besides I haven't passed the bar yet."

"What if you were slandered on TV and your girlfriend wouldn't talk to you because of it?"

"This is not advice, but even if you won, are you prepared to wait ten years."

"Ten years."

"The TV station is going to stall as long as they can, in the hope that you will run out of money, trying to pay your lawyer. This motion, that motion. They covered that in Torts and in Trial Law."

"It would be too late by then."

"At least you will have had your days and days in court."

"But what about my right to privacy?"

"Just be glad they didn't report that you were a drug dealer. The government would seize everything you have and call it ill-gotten gain. You'd be wiped out and have to go to the government for a lawyer."

"I thought it was one of those commandments that the government couldn't take you're stuff without a fair trial."

"Not anymore, I think Scalia wrote the majority opinion."

"So they could take away all the property of Echo Books and they wouldn't have to prove Ernie guilty of anything?"

"The IRS does it all the time."

"You're supposed to be innocent until proven guilty."

"Speaking of guilt before innocence, why are you putting the books in three different stacks?

Shouldn't it be two, the ones you want and those you don't."

"Nah, we take almost everything here. The first stack is for the best stuff, where we pay 25-30 per cent of the cover price. The next stack is the more marginal stuff, stuff that might not sell, and end up on the bargain table. The last stack is going straight to the bargain table."

"So you buy everything?"

"Unless it's falling apart, or filthy, or unsaleable for whatever reason."

"I'm glad most of my books are in the first stack."

"You brought in good books, strong feminist books. Mary Daly, Kate Millett, Andrea Dworkin and Adrienne Rich."

"You've read all those writers?"

"I've heard of them."

"Why did you put Robin Morgan's *Demon Lover*, in the second stack?"

"I'm not familiar with her and it's published by Norton, they publish a lot of textbooks. Textbooks date real fast."

"I never thought the publisher could determine the value of the book."

"Actually, we go by them all the time, we count on the editors to know what they're doing. Sometimes you can just look at the cover."

"You actually judge a book by the cover."

"Sure, you look at how it's illustrated, you look at the graphics and you look at the blurbs. If the best blurb on the cover is from the Dayton-Toledo Post-Gazette, you know something is up."

"Do you ever actually look in the books?"

"Sure, to see if they're defective, marked up, underlined, or highlighted. To see if it has a table of contents, an index or footnotes, what booksellers call the scholarly apparatus."

"I hope you read the titles."

"Sure, sometimes I'll even buy a book because it has a weird title. Take this one, *The Speculum of the Other Woman*, I have no idea what it means, but that doesn't matter, it's a great title."

"Irigaray."

"Excuse me?"

"The author of the book."

"Right. Well, here's the total." Mike handed her his scribbled calculation.

"It's more than I expected."

"Well with Powell's, Ogara's and Lou's in the neighborhood, Ernie feels like he has to compete for books."

"Whatever the reason, thanks."

"That's what I like, another satisfied customer, Ernie'd be proud." Mike muttered as he rang up the buy on the register.

"Here's your money, if you'll just sign the book here."

"Why do I have to sign?"

"Ernie says it's for tax reasons, but I suspect he also wants to make sure that there actually was a seller."

She signed the book and pushed the empty stroller out the door. Mike marked the books with Ernie's code that indicated who, when, where the books were bought, what was paid and where they should be shelved. He put the first two piles in the to be looked up spot. He pulled a book out of the third stack and put the stack on the floor, Ernie would want to look at them before they made it to the bargain table. He settled into the chair by the register and began to thumb through *The Social Origins of Private Life* by Stephanie Coontz.

Fifteen minutes later he heard some activity in the back, so he put the book down, and started to look up the books that he had bought. Ernie came up from the back.

"I'm glad to see you're doing something productive." Ernie said.

"Some woman came in and sold some books." Mike said.

"You know, Professor Weir called and said you underpaid him."

"We did the buy the same as always."

"Next time he comes in, I promised we would pay him the dollar."

"How could he tell I shorted him?"

"Something about the mathematical impossibility." Ernie surveyed the table. "These look quite good. Where are the bargain books?"

"Over here on the floor."

"Yes, these are definitely bargain books, she must have been very goodlooking."

"She was okay, but I think she was married."

"She may have been okay, but I'm not sure we are."

"Brian said you were doing some bookkeeping."

"Yes, well, it appears that we are going to lose money again this month, unless sales radically increase."

"Does that mean no bonus this month?"

"The part of the bonus that is based on gross sales will remain. But those parts based on increased sales and profit, obviously will not."

"How can you afford to give bonuses, if we're losing money?"

"I can't. I should never have set up the bonus system the way I did. I was naive."

"Sorry to hear that."

"Well, do what you can to boost sales."

"Sure thing."

"You realize of course, that if things continue as they are, or, God forbid, they get worse because of your notoriety, I may have to let you go."

"Don't worry that can't happen, I really need the money these days. I got to pay a month and a half rent on Sunday."

"Just so you know."

"You leaving?"

"Yes, I have some things to do. Kate should be here shortly. By the way, did she do anything Sunday that I should know about?"

"Not that I remember."

"Well, if anything unusual happens, let me know."

"I'll let you know."

"I will see tomorrow then."

"Later."

Ernie headed out into the twilight. After fifteen minutes, when Mike was sure that Ernie was really gone, he picked up the book again. He was reading it when Kate walked in.

"Hi Mike, what are you reading?" Kate asked.

"I'm not reading, I'm looking for a reference." Mike said.

"What are you referencing?"

Mike held up the book, "This woman was on NPR and she said that during colonial times it was legal to beat your wife with anything thinner than you thumb."

"I believe it."

"Yeah, me too, but the part I liked, she said that's where the expression 'rule of thumb' comes from. I thought I would check it out."

"Your fight with Nancy?"

"We never fight."

"Look it up in the index."

"It doesn't have an index."

"No index."

"You know sometimes these histories don't have indexes, like they're telling a story and they don't want you to skip to the good parts."

"I hate books without indexes, they're a pain, and besides it doesn't seem professional."
"I hate those bad indexes. All promises, and then you find that they only list the people mentioned and nothing else. You think the author makes up the index or maybe the publisher does?"
"Say what do you think those women are doing?"
"Which ones? Oh them -- they're students dressing up like peasants, probably members of that Society for Creative Anachronism."
"Well I'm going to see what's up." Kate said and went to talk to the women gathering in front of the store. Mike watched Kate through the front window as she spoke to several of the women. She seemed to be both understanding and confrontational. A half hour later, as dusk descended into night, Kate came back in.
"So what's the big deal?" Mike asked.
"They're Earthsters." Kate.
"What are Earthsters?"
"Oh, part of the whole Earthen movement. I think they're CSD."
"Okay, so what's CSD?"
"Coven of Satan's Daughters."
"Sounds like witches to me."

"I think they're more pagans. They have an office over in the Unitarian seminary."

"Isn't that the building that Prairie City Books is in?"

"Prairie City is in the basement. They have their office on the third floor. Meadville Theological Seminary, that's it."

"That's where Andrew works, I'll have to ask him about them. So what are they doing here anyway?"

"They're protesting the persecution of witchcraft."

"Why here?"

"Professor Gyula was lecturing on the Dark Arts."

"So."

"They feel that the only reason the police haven't arrested you, is because they condone the suppression of the occult."

"Why would they do that?"

"To support the patriarchy, of course. And of course the Earthsters support a return to the matriarchy."

"Mother Earth."

"The way it was before males ruined the world."

"Given a chance, I'm sure women could do the same thing."

"They want the chance."

"They can have it, as far as I'm concerned. As long as they let customers come in."

"I tried to convince them not to block the door."

"At least we'll have some customers, otherwise Ernie's going to be real unhappy."

"I made the argument that it was like an abortion clinic. Just because they're angry with the doctor, doesn't mean they should take it out on the desperate women, the customers."

"So you were saying, I was an abortionist."

"Mike, they think you are the murderer."

"Still, I'm not sure I like being called, you know, an abortionist."

"What's wrong with abortion?"

"Nothing. I just think the guy should have some say over what happens to his kid, that's all."

"You don't believe a woman has the right to control her own body?"

"I didn't say that. I can't believe it, they're starting to sing or something, I think I'm going to do some shelving in the back."

As the women linked hands, outside, and started to sing a hymn, Mike scurried to the back of the store. He hid in Social Science for most of the night. When the singing died down, he came up front.

"Hey Kate, you think they were sirens trying to draw me on to the rocks, so to speak."

"Mike, they haven't left."

Mike looked to the display windows and saw each one filled with women staring at him. He turned and discreetly checked his fly. Turning to Kate he asked, "And what do you think they're looking at?"

"You of course, who else."

"Yeah, but why are they staring like that."

"I don't know, probably giving you the evil eye."

"This is not good, you know any way I can stop them?"

"When I was a girl, we used to point devil horns at the bad guys, not that I can say it ever did any good."

"You mean where you hold your middle two fingers down with your thumb, like you were going give someone devil horns behind his back, yeah I did that as a kid."

"Well try it, it can't hurt."

Mike examined his hands, "which one should I start with, the left or the right?" Mike asked.

"I'd go with the right first, you can always switch." Kate suggested.

Mike held up the two fingers on his right hand. Nothing happened.

"So far so good, now point those fingers at them." "Like this?"
Mike pointed and swept his hand across all the windows, the staring stopped. The coven joined hands and began their hymn again.
"It's that same old song. But I'm not getting that evil eye, thanks Kate."
"No problem."
"For sure. Any idea how to get them to stop singing?"
"Quit."
"That's kind of a nasty thing to say."
"I know who I'm talking to."
Mike looked up at the windows, "Does that look like a Channel 7 van to you?"
"You mean one of those remote broadcast things?"
"Yeah, like that."
"I guess so."
"And that guy getting out of the van, does he look like Caesar Cortez?"
"It could be. I can't tell at this distance."
"I'd spot that guy from a mile away, he ruined my life. Nancy, now the witches, I could kill that guy."
"You are right! It is Caesar Cortez, I can't believe he's here."

"I believe it. Remind me not to watch the news."

"But he's a celebrity and in our store."

"He hasn't come in yet, and before he does, here are my keys."

"What am I supposed to do with your keys?"

"Lock up. I'm going out the back door. Witches are one thing, but reporters, that's something else."

"But Mike."

"Do the normal routine. It's not like we've been busy. If there is a problem, I'll straighten it out with Ernie in the morning."

"But what about you're end of day routine?"

"Do the same thing, but run it on the X key."

"Mike?"

"Act like I'm still here."

"But I don't know how to do any of that closing stuff."

"Do what you can, leave the rest, just be sure to lock the door."

"Okay, but I hope you know what you're doing."

"I know one thing for sure, I am out of here."

Chapter 8

"What are you doing here?" Brian asked, as Mike came into Robert's Roost.

"Drinking, hopefully, what did you think?" Mike answered.

"It's seven, the store doesn't close till eight."

"That Caesar Cortez guy showed up, so I had to leave."

"So you closed early?"

"Nah, I left Kate in charge."

"Of the store? To answer his questions?"

"Yeah, I gave her my keys."

"Your keys?"

"But don't worry, it's not like there were any customers."

"Of course there were customers."

"Not a single one. My guess is, witches scared them off."

"Kate's not a witch."

"No, seriously, there must have been a dozen witches outside protesting."

"Protesting what?"

"I think Kate said it was hate crime."

"Someday, you'll have to remind me why I hired you."

"Because I'm a nice guy. Boy, Peter and Fergie are sure going at it, down at the other end."

"That professor that's talking to Bela is more interesting."

"Yeah, who's he?"

"Vladimir Boyarescu, teaches over in the Divinity School."

"What's he teach?"

"Gnosticism."

"What's that."

"A pre-Christian cult thing."

"I hope he's not a Slovak."

"No, he's Romanian, an expert on the history of religion in Romania."

"Wasn't Gyula Rumanian?"

"Hungarian, but his lecture was on Transylvania. That's why Vlad hates Zoltan."

"I don't get it, isn't Transylvania in Hungary."

"The southern section of the Carpathian mountains used to belong to Hungary, now it's part of Romania."

"Let me guess, they speak Hungarian in Transylvania?"

"Exactly."

"Here we go again."
"Have some fun, listen in."
"The talk was a fourberie. The man was a cheat, a swindler. Worse, he was a charlatan, a quack, a poseur." Vladimir said.
"Nevertheless, for a life to end in such a simulacrum of the savage and the primitive." Bela countered.
"Certainly annihilation is the most virulent nihilism." Vladimir agreed.
"Ethnographically, the violent and the sacred are synonymous." Bela asserted.
"A congruence of gnosis, mythos and logos." Vladimir added.
"Yet, a most profane mise en scène."
"Extremely symbolic of evil."
"The stain, the defilement, the impure."
"Yet, defilement is not literally a stain nor impurity filthiness."
"Are we trying to recontextualize the problematic!" Bela snapped.
"Merely a contestation of whose normality reigns." Vladimir answered.
"My bête noire."
"I have no idea what those two are talking about." Mike said to Brian.

"Anthropologists, I love them." Brian said.
"But what are they talking about?"
"Zoltan, I think. You missed the good part, Bela said that History of Religion was just anthropology without the field work, and Vlad countered that anthropology would never survive the scrutiny of deconstruction and destructuralism."
"That may sound pretty good to you, but I'm going to talk to some real people. You make out anything else interesting, you let me know."
"Peter and Fergie?"
"Nah, Earl and Terry."
"The townies?"
"Yeah, the tradesmen. They're white trash, but I kind of like them."
"There's a big difference between working class and white trash, and besides Earl is black."
"I know that and you know that, but sometimes I'm not sure they know that."
"Just don't get into a fight, I'm not in the mood to back you up."
"Not my cohort tonight, I can see that."
"Not part of your cohort."
"Well, later." Mike turned and walked down the bar. The tradesmen were sitting in the middle of the

bar, Fergie and Peter were at the end. Mike paused in the middle and Earl spotted him.

"How's it going Mike?" Earl said.

"Fine, yourself?" Mike answered.

"Okay, I guess. Hey, pull up a stool, maybe you can help us out with something. At what temperature should beer be served at?" Earl asked.

"Cold, I guess, but here it depends if the coolers are working."

"That's right, as cold as you can get." Terry said.

"Mike, you know Terry and Bart don't you? I don't need to introduce you, do I?" Earl asked.

"Terry's the painter and Bart's the carpenter, if my memory serves me." Mike said.

"That's right, and now a trick question, what do I do?"

"You're an electrician."

"Yep, your memory is still there."

"Personally, I like my beer on the cool side of room temperature, you get the fullest flavor." Bart said.

"Is that why you always stick your thumb in your beer?" Earl asked.

"Yeah, it's a old brew-master trick. They used to use their thumb to make sure the temperature was just right."

"What has that got to do with your beer?"

"Just keeping up the tradition I suppose."

"For myself, I like it cold, but not ice cold."

"Give me ice cold any day." Terry said.

"I suppose if I drank the swill they have on tap, I'd want it as cold a possible too." Bart said.

"What's wrong with Alterbrew?" Terry asked.

"Hey guys, I think I figured it out. If you drink the good stuff, your Pilsner or Heinekens, you want it warm, you drink Bud or Old Style, you want it medium cold, and if you drink the stuff on tap, you just might want it real cold." Mike said.

"Alterbrew is good cold." Terry said.

"That's just what I was saying, and besides alcohol is alcohol." Mike said.

"Whatever gets you through the night." Bart said.

"We got trouble, that looks like Mel to me." Earl said.

As Mel passed by, he leaned over and said, "Hey Mike, I just wanted to thank you. I thought I was losing her, but when that reporter came on TV, she just melted into my arms. It was like taking candy from a baby."

"Just don't ask me to do it again." Mike said.

"If alcohol is alcohol, then I suppose guns are guns?" Bart asked Mike.

"Exactly."

"I take it you don't know much about guns either."

"Hey, I know they both can kill you."

"Do you know the difference between a .22 and a .45?"

"I know the Mafia uses a .22 and the KGB uses a .25."

"Any idea why."

"Sylvester didn't say."

"Sylvester, not that moron that comes in here?"

"I don't think he's such an idiot and he knows all sorts of military things."

"Next time ask him what the difference between a .22 and a .45 is."

"It's size or something like that isn't it?"

"Diameter of a bullet or shell."

"In inches?"

"Yes."

"So your .25 caliber bullet is really just a quarter inch in diameter?"

"Something like that."

"Gyula was lucky he wasn't shot by a .45, that'd be almost half an inch in diameter."

"That professor over at the University?"

"Yeah, that's the one."

"He's dead, isn't he?"
"Yeah, so?"
"What difference does it make? Dead is dead."
"Wouldn't a half inch bullet make a bigger hole?"
"Yeah, but so what."
"He stood more of a chance."
"Maybe you got a point. The mob hit that guy in Chinatown, ricocheted off his skull and didn't kill him. In fact that's probably why he ended up testifying against them." Bart said.
"Yeah, getting shot would sure rankle my feathers." Mike said.
"Mine too." Earl said.
"So maybe the mob hit that professor?" Mike said.
"Did they find the gun?" Bart asked.
"I don't think so." Mike said.
"Well, then, it wasn't a mob hit. They always use a cheap .22 with a silencer, and they always drop it at the scene."
"What if somebody else picked it up?" Mike asked.
"Nobody would be that stupid."
"Sylvester seemed to think that it was a .25."
"It would be hard to tell, unless they found a spent cartridge, then it would be easy."

"So what's the difference, anyway."

"Your .22 goes faster, and although it doesn't have as much power, the .25 packs more of a punch."

"That doesn't sense, make how can a less powerful bullet have more punch."

"It's not the speed of the slug that counts, it's what it does on impact." Bart said.

"Like less is more, I like that." Mike said.

"Hey, don't knock .25s. I got my wife a .25 auto for protection. You never know when some creep is going to come around looking for trouble." Terry said.

"I suppose you bought her something cheap?" Bart said.

"Hey, I bought her a Sterling .25 auto with the satin nickel finish, you got a problem with that?" Terry said.

"I got mine a pearl-handled Bauer. I was going to get her a Baby Browning, but I decided to buy American." Bart said.

"Hey Bartender, a round of Alterbrew for my buddies and me." Terry called out.

"What's a Raven like?" Mike asked.

"Another cheap gun." Bart said.

"I think Peter said something about getting Magda one." Mike said.

"Not the gun to get your wife, if you plan to stay married." Bart said.

"Yeah, I think they may be having their problems these days, but you didn't hear it from me." Mike said.

"I heard his wife whacked him with a rolling pin. Why would you want to give a gun to a woman like that?" Terry said.

"I think he was worried about the neighborhood, crime, that kind of thing." Mike said.

"He's just asking for trouble." Terry said.

"Most murders are actually between people that know each other, you know, like husbands and wives. Terry may have a point, it's hard to believe, I know." Bart said.

"Just keep it down, he might hear you." Mike nodded at the end of the bar. "Pete's over there, talking to Fergie."

Bart and Terry looked down the bar. Earl looked at his beer, shook his head and smiled. They all listened.

"You owe me man." Fergie said to Petr.

"I pay, I pay. But first I must talk to my friends." Petr said.

"If I don't see some money by Friday, you know who I'll come looking for, that will be you."

"I talk to my buddies, they tell me what to do."

"I don't want to hurt you man, but I got to take care of business, if you know what I mean."
"Your wife and childrens."
"Yeah, Peter, you could look at it like that."
"Sorry, he's caught-up with Fergie, I doubt he heard anything." Mike said.
"Bunch of losers, if you ask me." Terry said.
"He owns a bunch of buildings. He owns my place over on Cornell, and he owns the building that Echo Books is in." Mike said.
"That other guy's always playing some game with somebody, and it's always trouble. I don't care what the game is, just trouble." Bart said.
"He's pretty much a regular at the bookstore." Mike said.
"He is? Well, take may advice and steer clear of him."
"Maybe I shouldn't of let him use the phone."
"He was probably calling his dealer." Terry said.
"Nah, he was calling God about a chess game." Mike said.
"I believe it, he is crazy." Bart said.
"Brian thinks it's the drugs." Mike said.
"I wonder. Maybe he is medicating his self." Earl said.
"His self always seems different." Terry said.

"You think he knows he's crazy?" Mike asked.
"Nah, it's the drugs." Bart said.
"Maybe he just uses drugs to control the craziness, you know like we all get crazy sometime." Earl said.
"I know what you mean, this week has been driving me crazy. I got witches protesting outside the store." Mike said.
"Shoot them. Get yourself a good old shotgun and blow those witches back down to the stone age." Terry said.
"I can't do that." Mike said.
"Sure you can. Just be sure to kill them, then you can say it was self-defense." Terry said.
"What are the witches mad at you for?" Bart asked.
"They think I killed that Gyula guy over at the University." Mike said.
"I bet it was self-defense." Earl said.
"Shouldn't surprise them none then, when you kill 'em." Terry said.
"Not my style. Sorry guys."
"Get Fergie then. He'll do anything for a buck." Bart said.
"I thought you said he was crazy." Mike said.

"Yeah, I bet he's crazy enough to be killing people." Earl said.

"Hey, Fergie," Bart shouted, "Come over here, Mike has a deal for you."

Fergie got up from the end and approached the middle of the bar. "So what's the deal?" Fergie asked.

"Nothing, Bart was just kidding." Mike asked.

"Mike has got a problem with too many witches. They're harassing him at work. I thought you might able to help him out. The big baby is afraid to shoot them himself." Bart said.

"Sounds like an interesting proposition. However, I'm expecting some of my, ah, investments to come in, in the next few days, so I doubt I will be in that market for some time to come." Fergie said.

"Thanks, Fergie." Mike said.

"No problem, always a pleasure to deal with you." Fergie said.

"No help at all." Bart said.

"I do what I can," Fergie turned to Petr's corner of the bar, "and Peter, I'll see you on Friday, I'm sure. Nice talking to you folks, but I must be going."

"Thanks for the help Bart." Mike said.

"Hey, you brought it up, I was just trying to help out." Bart said.

"Come on, there are other ways of dealing with people you don't like."

"With witches?"

"Anybody. Besides, how do you know that bullets could kill a witch. Don't you have to shoot a vampire with a silver bullet. In the old days they burned witches at the stake, right. They didn't put them in front of a firing squad."

"Who cares. You don't want to shoot 'em, then don't shoot 'em." Terry said.

"You torch his place, Peter is going to be one unhappy Polack, that's for sure." Bart said.

"Slovak."

"Slovenian, Croatian, Serbian, who cares, I wouldn't mess with them. Look what's happening over there now, they're killing each other and they've been doing that for thousands of years."

"I'm not going to burn down Echo Books, I'd probably lose my job."

"Why don't you ask Peter if some of his Serbian buddies could help you out?"

"Maybe I will, nice talking to you." Mike grinned, moved down the bar and sat next to Petr.

"How goes it with you." Petr asked.

"Not so good, we got witches protesting down by the store." Mike said.

"Why they do that?"

"They think I killed Zoltan Gyula, you know that professor over by the University. It was in the paper."

"Hungarian garbage, as bad as Czechs. He try to make trouble for my young country."

"I heard something about a dam?"

"That is right. We are poor country. We need energy to grow. He say no, save little fishes. Nobody eats those fishes. So all Slovaks suffer and little fishes they laugh at us."

"That's why the Greens don't want the dam?"

"Yes, it would upset poor little fishes."

"Maybe the fish are good for the river."

"Those fishes is good bait, I tell you that. They go, we use worms. We got good worms."

"I prefer artificial lures, myself, like your chartreuse and silver little cleo, for those cohos, oh boy, that is really something."

"You no powerline, with fire extinguisher."

"Nah, I just cast from the rocks, over by 51st Street."

"Cohos, you must powerline."

"I catch my share, besides I really don't like catching them. I just like going out there, on a nice day of course, and casting."

"My brother say you no fish. You bring beer with you. Maybe you fish."

"I like hanging out with nature, you know and besides the fall ain't the time to get your cohos."

"Try snagging"

"Actually, I'm more concerned about those witches."

"Maybe, my Magda is witch?"

"Mrs. Prst?"

"Sure. She bewitch me with her charms. Make me marry her. I wonder sometimes."

"You're probably just mad because she went dancing with Gyula."

"I no mad."

"I know I was kind of angry when Nancy went dancing with him. I figured you might be too."

"Okay, I angry, but we straighten out."

"So what about the witches in front of the store?"

"Who cares?"

"They're hurting business Don't you get a percentage of Ernie's gross?"

"Businessmens, they lie. They lie to government, they lie to me. I say what rent is and they pay. I see money, okay."

"I suppose you're wondering where the rent is."

"Yours? No problem buddy, I sure I see by Sunday."

"Or else."

"Sure. I must be businessman too, you know."

"About those witches."

"You kill that filth, I got no problem with that."

"But. . . ."

"You know what sewer look like when it back up in basement, is what I think of Hungarian."

"I was kind of hoping the Hlinka Guards could help out Ernie?"

"How you know Hlinka Guard?"

"I was thinking that if Ernie doesn't make any money, he won't be able to pay the rent."

"Yes and how you know Hlinka Guard?"

"Brian said something about the Guards and World War Two."

"My father was Captain in Hlinka Guards"

"So that's why you were persecuted by the Communists."

"Hitler give us our country back to us, after thousand years."

"Didn't you have to become a Nazi?"

"He say it was like Sokol or how you say, Boy Scouts."

"But didn't they have a thing against Jews?"

"Jew just rich Democrat."

"Okay, you don't like Democrats."

"Those Jews. When first I come to country, I work as janitor for Weiss and Schwarz. Over on 55th. Good old Amos and Saul. They pay me nothing, treat me like Czech. But I save my money, I buy buildings, now I in charge."

"Irregardless, that fascism stuff was pretty bad."

"Fasces is sticks and axe, what so bad about that?"

"I'm talking about that political thing, you know Mussolini and all that."

"Ah, fascismus."

"That's it."

"Fascimus is thousand points of light."

"I'm afraid I don't get you."

"Country, love or leave."

"That was a Vietnam thing."

"Man protects family, his people and country."

"You're not trying to say that America is fascist?"

"Of course. Your president, Kennedy was his name. He say 'Ask not what country do for you, ask what you do for country'. That is fascismus. You love your peoples."

"You know I never looked at it like that, but what about those witches?"
"I talk to my buddies, no problem."

Chapter 9

Mike came into Echo Books through the back door, the way he had left it the night before.

"Gee, Brian, there're more witches out there than yesterday." Mike said.

"And I thought you were kidding." Brian said.

"How'd Kate do?"

"She did nothing but lock up."

"Hey, that's what counts."

"Yep, but the boss isn't happy."

"Because I didn't count out the register?"

"Kate left all the money in the register, checks, everything."

"Look at those witches. What would you have done?"

"In any case, it's your lucky day, the Jesus Defense League is mounting a counter-demonstration."

"Yeah?"

"The people on Kimbark are all JDL, those on 53rd are CSD."

"You know, you ought stop speaking in code sometime." Mike said.

"Coven of Satan's Daughters." Brian said.

"That's better. You know those people on Kimbark look a lot like the folks that were over by the Oriental Institute. Remember, when we were going to the DAF book sale?"

"Protesting Zoltan's talk, I remember."

"Maybe they'll scare off the witches."

"I hope so, we could use some customers, but I kind of doubt it. They didn't scare Zoltan, he gave the talk"

"Maybe they should have scared him off, somebody sure did."

"I just hope we don't have some sort of incident."

"At least today they're not blocking the door."

"You think big, Mike."

"Just doing my job."

"Right. Why don't you take over the register, I'm going to find something to do in back. I need a breather from that crowd."

"Where's Ernie?"

"He disappeared about an hour ago, I have no idea where he went."

"Who's on the special today?"

"Didn't check the sign again I see. Let's see, if I remember correctly, it's Bill Mauldin, James Boswell,

Goebbels and Pope John Paul I. But somehow I don't think you'll have to worry about it."

"Don't think the witches will be buying John Paul, you're probably right."

"I'll be in the back if you need me." Brian said.

"Maybe the JDL will." Mike said. Mike sat at the register for three hours without a customer. He tried to distract himself by skimming through the new arrivals. They were mostly the feminist books he had bought on Tuesday. He ended up painfully bored and twiddling his thumbs. A heavy set figure blocked the doorway and pushed his way into the store.

"Hey, Andrew, what's up, you leave early?" Mike asked.

"No, I'm taking a break, I came down to see how you were doing." Andrew said.

"Oh, fine."

"Little bit of commotion outside, I happened to notice as I was coming in here."

"It's the battle of the C's."

"The Order of the C?" Andrew asked.

"Nah, the Christian something versus the Coven something." Mike answered.

"So it's not like it's a University thing."

"Everything is a University thing. Hyde Park is a company town."

"My point exactly, don't mess with the University."

"If the University hadn't invited Gyula, none of this would have happened."

"You can't blame them, just because the Slovaks or the Hlinkas had him assassinated."

"They found the killer?"

"Not exactly, but that's the consensus of everyone that I've talked to."

"How am I ever going to convince that coven that it was the Slovaks."

"Leave it to the FBI and the CIA, after all, isn't that why we pay taxes."

"Maybe Tony was right, I wish they could just lock them all up."

"What? Well, anyway, that's not why I came. I thought you might like to know that Ernie just created a real big fuss over at Prairie City."

"What'd he do?"

"Tried to get Woody to convince the president of Meadville to terminate the lease on that office space that the Coven rents."

"Going to bat for me, all right."

"I think Freundlich was going for it, but wouldn't you know it, Jack Shone, the minister over at First Unitarian, he shows up. Talk about timing."

"So."

"So, the conversation got so heated and loud, they had to take it upstairs, probably to one of the classrooms."

"What could Shone have said?"

"Well Ernest got Woodrow to argue to President Freundlich that the Coven was stifling the free speech of Hyde Park, by suppressing people's ability to buy books. Woody could argue that wholeheartedly, I'm sure it didn't take much convincing on Ernie's part."

"So what did this Shone guy say?"

"Oh, he showed up and argued that witches had their own rights to free speech. That's to be expected of course. The part I liked, too bad I missed the rest of it, was when he went on about being an inclusive ministry that welcomes everyone in the community. That really ticked the President off, he made a big deal about the difference between a congregation and a community. That's when they went upstairs. I gather, and you didn't hear this from me, that some of the more conservative churches have been giving him a lot of grief. Unhappy with what's coming out of the seminary, even complaining to Boston, that's where they have their headquarters."

"Maybe, I'll write a letter myself."

"I didn't think you were Unitarian Universalist."

"I'm not, but if they'll include anybody, then they can include me too."

"Write them, then. Wasn't it Groucho Marx who said 'I would never join a club that would have someone like me as a member'?"

"Me neither. You think it'll do any good?"

"The letter? I doubt it."

"Woody talking to Freundlich."

"I just hope Woody doesn't do anything that could jeopardize my job, such as it is these days."

"I take that to be a no."

"An optimistic no."

"Not to change the subject or anything, but are there any openings over a Prairie City?"

"You mean jobs?"

"Yeah."

"Probably mine, after Woodrow and Penelope get finished with my mushroom treatment."

"Besides that."

"Students come and go. You never know. The one you want to talk to is Woody, only don't call him Woody, call him Mr. Beech or Woodrow, until he asks you to call him Woody."

"But everybody calls him Woody."

"Do you want to be a customer or an employee, it's a power thing."

"Sounds pretty neurotic to me."

"Every Hyde Park bookseller is neurotic, I'm sure Ernie has his fair share of neuroses, believe me."

"I guess they're different kinds."

"Why did you ask anyway? You seem perfectly at home here."

"I guess I am. But hard work and no pay, that might make me want to leave home."

"Ernie's's not paying his employees."

"With no customers, how can he?"

"Still, after taxes, maybe rent, you have to pay the people that sell the goods."

"The guy thinks suicide is a good thing."

"Why?"

"Helps him get to sleep."

"See what did I tell you. If he needs that to get him to sleep, he's got more problems then I ever want to deal with."

"Me too. So you think there might be an opening at Prairie?"

"Like I said, talk to Woodrow."

"Maybe I will."

"Well, I better get back to work, these days I'm not sure they'd appreciate my long lunch break."

"Later, Andrew."

Relunctantly, Mike settled back into his routine, when Magda walked in with Bonney.
"All right, some customers." Mike exclaimed.
"Hey Mike, I thought I'd help Magda pick out some books." Bonney said.
"We got in some good feminist stuff recently."
"I was thinking more domestic abuse, that sort of thing."
"If we have anything, it would be in the health section."
"Not in the family section?"
"We don't have a family section. The self-help kind of stuff would be in Health. The social work stuff would be in Social Science."
"I guess we want the health section then."
"You don't find anything, be sure to check out the new arrivals."
"Thanks Mike."
"No problem."
Bonney and Magda chatted amiably, as they browsed the health section and then moved to the new arrivals. Mike stared into space with a benign smile. An hour later, they returned to the register.
"It sure is quiet in here today." Bonney said.
"The folks outside are scaring some folks off." Mike said.

"What's up with those guys anyway?"
"Protesting because of Gyula's death."
"Just because of that news story on Channel Seven, remember, with Caesar Cortez?"
"Yeah, I remember. I'm afraid so."
"That's just ridiculous."
"Bonney who are those peoples?" Magda asked.
"Mike?"
"In front, those are the witches, and on the side, those would be the Christians." Mike explained.
"Witches, you know my grandmother always put thumb in fist to protect from witch and ghost." Magda said.
"Well, my grandmother claimed that holding your left thumb in your right hand would cure the hiccups." Bonney said.
"I just might try that." Mike said.
"It never worked for me." Bonney said.
"I mean Mrs. Prst's witch cure. I know that they really can't hurt me, but it can't hurt to play it safe, just in case."
"Remember, you must do with both hands." Magda reminded.
"Like this?"
"Yes, that is it."
"Thanks. So did you ladies find anything?"

"I picked out *The Speculum of the Other Woman*, and Robin Morgan's *The Demon Lover*. I thought Magda might want to start *The Second Sex*." Bonney answered.

"Teaching her to be an American. Excellent choices. I had my eye on both of those myself." Mike said.

"There may be hope for you yet."

"Yeah, now that I talked to Mrs. Prst. You know, I don't know how I can possibly ring up your books."

"Undo your fist, and use your fingers."

"I can't do that just now, it might break the spell. Why don't you ladies take the books, and I'll collect for them at the bar, okay."

"It's your job to lose."

"Yeah, I know."

"Such a nice man." Magda added.

"Come on, Magda. See you later Mike." Bonney said.

"Thanks Mrs. Prst. Thanks for the tip. I'm sure it'll work." Mike said.

"Maybe I see you later." Magda said.

"Come on Magda."

"Thanks again." Mike said.

"I must go."

"Later."

Mike settled back into his chair. As he grew impatient, he looked down at his fists and realized he couldn't twiddle his thumbs. At five, Kate came in.

"Gee I'm sure glad to see you." Mike said.

"I doubt that." Kate said.

"Seriously, I was getting kind of antsy, sitting here with nothing to do."

"No one's come in because of the protest."

"We haven't sold a single book."

"What am I going to do all night."

"That's what I was asking myself."

"What's wrong with your hands."

"Mrs. Prst says it might scare those witches away."

"It looks pretty neurotic to me. Besides the Earthsters have a right to protest what they see as a legitimate grievance."

"Yeah, well what would you recommend, Your Ms. Politically Correct Highness?"

"In Irish, Celtic, mythology there's Finn of the Phantoms." Kate volunteered.

"So this Quinn guy, how did he handle witches?" Mike asked.

"Finn. To understand his dreams, handle problems or see into the future, he would bite his thumb with his tooth of wisdom. He even foresaw his own death."

"Yeah, well, I don't want to understand my dreams and I certainly don't want to know how I'm going to die."

"Maybe you could do something about it. You ever think about that."

"It would take the mystery out of living. Besides, I had my wisdom teeth pulled, they were bony and impacted."

"You think it's funny, but it's not. I should have known better than take a job where women were in the minority."

"Like I'm responsible how my teeth grew."

"The oppressors can't speak for the oppressed."

"Huh?"

"The attack of the power structure on the oppressed. Family values, ever hear of that?"

"Yeah, so what."

"There's no way a male could even comprehend what it's like to be an Irish woman in this sexist society."

"The mayor is Irish."

"Do you know that only five percent of the city is Irish? It scares me just to think about it."

"So what are you, an oppressed woman, or an oppressed Irish."

Rule of Thumb

"Give Ireland back to the Irish, and then get rid of those silly laws."

"If you had to choose between the part of you that is Irish -- which means you'd have to real Catholic and be against abortion and all -- and you as a woman -- which means you would want to be pro-choice, which would you choose, that's what I'd like to know."

"I'd join the coven and force you to think, for the first time in your life, I suspect."

"Me, I'd probably go with what I thought was best for me. Forget that clique stuff. That would be like being in a gang, or a Unitarian or something. All these people they feel like they got to be part of some group."

"You're known by who you hang out with, I have to agree. But you see, that's the way discrimination works. Before you even do that, people assume you have."

"So when I assumed you were donating your paycheck to the IRA, I was discriminating."

"Exactly, I only tithe."

"That's a relief."

"You made a false assumption."

"So I shouldn't assume those witches are all that bad."

"You can't understand them, you're male."

"I was just thinking, what if I was a witch or a warlock, what would I do if Professor Gyula died? Maybe I'd protest too."

"Mike you can't imagine what it's like to be one of the oppressed."

"I could try."

"Your cultural training precludes it."

"I guess I'll shelve then."

"If you keep holding your hands like that, then it's probably the only thing you can do."

"Hey, and don't worry about last night."

"I wasn't, I did what you told me to do."

"Yeah, well before he left, Brian said Ernie was in one of his moods. If he gives you any trouble, you just tell him he can talk to me."

"I'll definitely do that."

"Well, I'm going to do some shelving, anybody comes in to sell books, give me a holler."

"Have fun."

Mrs. Mondevi walked into the store around seven. There was a twinkle in her pale blue eyes and the lines about her eyes formed a smile.

"I'm glad we finally have a customer." Kate said.

"I normally come in on Sundays, but I wanted to see how Mack was dealing with the sisters." Mrs. Mondevi said.

"You mean Mike?"

"The young man with the mustache and short dark hair parted down the middle."

"Yes, that's Mike, and I'm afraid he's not taking it well."

"Hey, I heard that." Mike said as he stepped up to the register. Turning, he said "How you doing, Mrs. Mondevi?"

"Fine. I just came over to see how you were doing with the Coven of Satan's Daughters." Mrs. Mondevi said.

"My hands are tied, as you can see."

"That's supposed to scare off those girls?"

"That's what Magda said."

"I seriously doubt that will help."

"So what am I supposed to do?"

"Nothing. They're just children."

"They were giving me the evil eye."

"You could always expectorate. If that doesn't work, I have a necklace of cowry shells."

"I'm not wearing a necklace."

"But you are willing to hold your hands in that silly position."

"Yeah, well, Magda, she's from the old country."

"Old? Medieval, at best."

"The middle ages is pretty old."

"It has been modern for the last 5000 years, at the very least."

"I thought the 20th century was modern?"

"To my mind, the modern age begins with the dawn of the patriarchy."

"Patriarchy?"

"Yeah, that's when men started to ruin things." Kate explained.

"Thanks, Kate." Mike said.

"As I was saying, by naming themselves the Daughters of Satan, they are just playing into the patriarchy." Mrs. Mondevi said.

"How so?" Mike asked.

"By making a male figure, their symbol."

"Who? You mean the devil?"

"After all, the whole concept of Satan was invented by the Patriarchs of the Church to get rid of the women that led their communities."

"So these weird sisters out front, they really don't know what they're doing."

"Oh, they might have learned a few things, but I rather doubt it."

"Watch that talk about the devil, I heard somewhere that if you speak of the devil, he'll either come himself or send somebody else." Kate warned.
    "She is right, you know." Mrs. Mondevi said.
    "I didn't bring it up." Mike said.
    "You know, Mike, you could always cross yourself, maybe that would work." Mrs. Mondevi suggested.
    Mike crossed himself.
    "No, I guess that didn't." Mrs. Mondevi said.
    "Now they're crossing themselves in some sort of pagan way." Mike said.
    "I've got an authentic Celtic Cross at home." Kate said.
    "That might help, dear," Mrs. Mondevi said to Kate and turned to Mike, "Why don't you try what they were doing?"
    "I don't know any witchcraft." Mike said.
    "Of course, you do. Here, let me show you." She grasped Mike's right hand and directed it. "You touch your left breast like this, then your forehead, your right breast, now your left shoulder, right shoulder, that's right, and back to your left breast. That's it."
    "I don't see why the Star of David would scare them." Mike said.
    "It looked like a Druid's Foot to me." Kate said.

"It is an extremely common symbol, hence something those girls might understand." Mrs. Mondevi answered.

"Sounds good to me, let me try that again. Left chest, forehead, right chest, left shoulder, and then what?" Mike said.

"Right shoulder, and back to the starting point."

"I think I got it."

"You are doing fine."

"Hey, and look they don't seem so pleased with themselves, no more."

"No, but they're spray painting the windows with pentagrams." Kate observed.

"Some of them have those markers. Kate, you want to talk them and explain how defacing property with signs is against the law in Chicago?" Mike suggested.

"I talked to them last night, it's your turn."

"I will talk to the children." Mrs. Mondevi volunteered.

"Thanks Mrs. Mondevi." Mike said.

"My pleasure."

Mrs. Mondevi shuffled out the door and into the crowd.

"She's really chewing them out." Mike said.

"I've never seen her so animated." Kate said.

"She's better than the JDL."

The group outside began to disperse. Mrs. Mondevi came back into the store.

"That was great." Mike said.

"What did you say to them?" Kate asked.

"I merely pointed out that, during the middle ages, the pentacle was a sign of protection. So that when the put the sign of the pentacle on the store, to protect themselves from Mack. . . ." Mrs. Mondevi said.

"Mike." Mike said.

"Yes, well, whatever, they were actually protecting the store from any outside evil."

"Brilliant."

"So that's why they left?" Kate asked.

"Of course. That, and I pointed out to them that it was eight o'clock and the store would be closing shortly." Mrs. Mondevi said.

"Well done."

"Speaking of closing, maybe we should wrap things up, if you know what I mean, what do say?" Mike asked Kate.

"Mike, I think I'll walk Mrs. Mondevi home, if that's okay with her, and you."

"Thank you, you are such a dear." Mrs. Mondevi said.

"Yeah sure, and leave me stranded, to count out the register and all the other stuff." Mike said.
"You can handle it. Good night." Kate said.
"Good night." Mrs. Mondevi said.
"Good night, ladies."
The store was empty, Mike locked the front door, opened the register and muttered, "Women."

Chapter 10

"What's Brian doing with the widow?" Mike asked John as he walked into the bar.

"I know. I saw that. She's working through her grief, in the strangest way." John said.

"Brian's not so strange."

"No, I mean, after the death of her husband, she has become really quite promiscuous."

"What's wrong with that, as long as that gets her over it. You now, whatever works."

"Mind you, not that I have anything against promiscuity per se."

"You think Mrs. Gyula is putting a move on Brian?"

"I think, maybe, he's out of his league."

"Brian can handle himself, besides, I think it's been a while."

"That's what scares me."

"Be good for him to have something to relate to besides his tropical fish."

"I'm just concerned, because she's from a much larger pond than Brian."

"Los Angeles isn't so much bigger than Chicago."

"I was thinking more like Hyde Park."

"Oh, I see what you mean. Yeah, it's bigger than Hyde Park."

"In addition, there are all those other worlds that Zoltan investigated."

"Yeah, Italy."

"Ah, right."

"In that case, I think I'll join the Peggys and see if I can figure out what kind of fish this Meg Gyula is."

"Peggys? Who are the Peggys?"

"Rita, Gretchen, and Marjorie. You know, the Lab School teachers. I call them the Peggys."

"I know who they are, they taught my children, and not one is named Peggy."

"Same difference, except Marjorie's not with them."

"Whatever that means."

"I'll let you know if I learn anything."

"Impress me."

"I'll do my best."

"Remember now, the Peggys, as you refer to them, are all single women in their thirties. You may be a small fish, yourself, in that pond."

"I'm just looking out for Brian, that's all."

Rule of Thumb

"Just be careful."

"I'm already spoken for, Nancy-wise, so there's no problem there."

"Yes, I'm sure, go mingle."

"Thanks John." Mike said and strolled down the bar.

"Hi, Mike, would you care to join us?" Gretchen asked.

"Be glad to, ladies." Mike said.

"What did you do to your thumb?" Rita asked.

"Nothing. Magda said it might scare those witches away." Mike answered.

"You know what it means, don't you?" Gretchen asked.

"It means I'm desperate." Mike said.

"No, if you hold your thumb like that, when you make a fist, that means your not so sure of yourself. And uncomfortable around other people too." Gretchen said.

"Besides that, if you punch somebody, you could break your thumb. Safer to keep it on the outside." Rita said.

"In which case, you'd be strong-tempered and strong-willed." Gretchen added.

"I just want the witches to leave the store. So I can get paid on Sunday." Mike said.

"My, this is interesting. Mike, do you think all women are witches?" Gretchen asked.

"I hate to change the subject, Mike, but do you know all the professors at the U of C?" Rita asked.

"Mostly, just Pasteelle and Goodgame. They're more Brian's friends than mine, any how. But I know them." Mike said.

"What do you talk about?" Rita asked.

"Sports, the usual stuff."

"It looked like they were staring at Brian."

"What's he up to now?" Mike said, turning to the bar. "He's giving her the fraternity handshake, I can't believe it."

"No, no. They're thumb wrestling." Rita said

"What's that?" Gretchen asked.

"That's when two people hold their fingers together, and then try hold the other person's thumb down with their's."

"I'll put a dime on Brian." Mike said.

"I'll take that bet." Rita said.

"I wonder what it's all about?" Gretchen asked.

"They're flirting, that's all." Rita said.

"The battle of the sexes, I just love it, it adds new meaning to the term 'opposable thumbs'." Gretchen said.

"Yeah, well I'm kind of concerned about Brian. He's up there flirting with Gyula's widow, and I was wondering what you guys made of her?" Mike asked.

"Who's that?" Rita asked.

"The woman that Brian's with, she's been sitting at your table, ever since she walked into the place."

"Oh, you mean Meg Furie Gyula." Rita said.

"Yeah, that's the one."

"She shares too much." Gretchen said.

"It's not that, it's that she trusts men." Rita corrected.

"There's that too, but there are some things, I'd just rather not know about." Gretchen said.

"She's having a rough time." Rita said.

"Her husband dying, that's what I figured." Mike said.

"Not only that, she has a sickly little girl." Rita said.

"You think it was Gyula's kid?" Mike asked

"Of course, whose else would it be?"

"Mama's baby, papa's maybe."

"She said she was a virgin when she got married."

"How long have they been married?"

"About two years. Gretchen, isn't that right?"

"A couple three years." Gretchen said.

"She's been around though, she must be close to forty?" Mike said.

"What has age got to do with it." Rita said.

"You'd just have to figure that an Italian woman would have lost her virginity by then." Mike said.

"She's not Italian. Come on, she has blond hair. She teaches at UCLA. She said she met her husband at a MLA conference." Rita said.

"A Californian. In that case, she probably lost it in high school." Mike said.

"From her description of their wedding night, I believe her. That's a pain you remember."

"It's painful enough that some ex-nuns, who've left their orders, when they were in their thirties, they tried it once and decided forget that, it's not for me." Gretchen added.

"I thought that in the heat of love, nobody noticed." Mike said.

"We can assume Nancy wasn't a virgin." Rita said.

"She might as well be." Mike muttered.

"You know, she told us you were a sexual Sesame Street." Rita said.

"She talked about that?" Mike asked.

"And 'Open Sesame'."

"I only tried that once."

"Girls talk."
"Cookie Monster?"
"What's wrong with Sesame Street?" Gretchen asked.
"It's for children. Sex is for adults." Rita said.
"But that's how grown-ups play." Gretchen said.
"You think she got pregnant, the one time she did it with Gyula?" Mike asked.
"I'd say she has gotten over it, and judging from her recent behavior, seems to enjoy it." Rita said.
"I got to ask Mel sometime." Mike said.
"Oh, good old Malcolm Hastscort III. Simply marvelous in bed, that's why it's such a pity that he has never had a single intelligent thing to say. Cuts down on the conversation when you're not. . . ." Gretchen said.
"I can't stand the guy myself." Rita said.
"Me neither, but you have to admire his persistence." Mike said.
"He acts like he's the only male guppy in this goldfish bowl." Rita said.
"I see you know your fish, you should talk to Brian some time, I think he's experimenting with Cichlids these days." Mike said.
"His fish are sick?" Gretchen asked.
"It's a type of fish, like Angelfish." Rita explained.

"I think Gretchen's got it right, he's got some sort of problem with his tank, kills all his fish, sooner or later." Mike said.

"Probably Ich." Rita said.

"You're not suggesting that Brian has an icky pond?" Gretchen asked.

"Ich, is a protozoa that infects fish, some sort of Greek louse." Rita said.

"Sounds German to me." Mike said.

"No, it's definitely Greek." Rita said.

"But Herr Strausskopf said." Mike protested.

"Ichthyophthirius, from the Greek, phtheir, meaning louse, which is what you are quickly becoming."

"Hey, believe me, I'm no Mel."

"Well, I don't admire your persistence."

"But we were just talking."

"You never talk to us. Go back to your buddies, I don't know why you tried to sit with us, unless it was to try and protect your so-called friend."

"Brian, he's busy. Well, I can see that I'm not wanted here anymore, maybe I'll find myself a spot at the bar."

"Good night Mike, nice talking to you again." Gretchen said.

"'Night Gretchen, Rita." Mike said and moved to the bar.

"What a jerk, why did you invite him to our table?" Rita said.

"He looked lonely somehow." Gretchen said.

"I wish you would stop playing games with Nancy." Rita said.

"Who's playing games with whom?" Gretchen asked.

Mike stopped eavesdropping, and settled into a stool. He raised his hand and caught Kaz's eye. "Kaz, another Old Style, when you get a chance."

"How's it going buddy?" Kaz asked.

"Same old bad, bad same old." Mike answered.

"You and me both."

"Has Nancy been here tonight?"

"Not on my shift. But then she might have been in here earlier. Who am I to say?"

"Yeah, I haven't seen much of her, either. You seen Tony around?"

"Speak of the devil." Kaz turned. "What can I get for you, Officer Grata?"

"I'll take an Old Style." Grata said.

"Coming right up."

"How was work?" Mike asked.

"Saved some folks on Harper from vicious dogs."

"Oh, yeah?"

"They were on their porch and snarling at them."

"What'd you do?"

"They were just two strays looking for a place to spend the night."

"And?"

"I told the folks to get inside their screen-door, and I went down and walked around and started to climb up the side of the porch."

"They didn't try to bite you?"

"They snarled but I had my flashlight out."

"So you clobbered them."

"No, they ran off. They were just scared. End of story and everybody was happy."

"I hope Brian and Meg don't have that problem?"

"They're leaving now." Kaz said.

"How's that?" Tony asked.

"Spending the night." Mike said.

"I hope Brian don't get in trouble." Kaz said.

"Who's the dame?" Tony asked.

"Meg, Meg Gyula. Remember, she came in with the Gnome on Monday night." Mike answered.

"The widow of the victim?"

"Yeah, it's weird."

"Not that weird, different people react differently, when it comes to grief. Some laugh, like a hysterical kind of laugh."

"Since you brought it up, how's the case going?"

"What, the Gyula assassination?"

"Yeah, that's the one I had in mind."

"You know I can't talk about police business, especially an active investigation."

"That's never stopped you before."

"Kaz, get Mike another beer."

"I should be buying you one."

"Coming right up." Kaz said.

"So what's the scoop?" Mike asked.

"Can't do it this time." Tony said.

"Please, it's really messing with my life."

"Rules are rules."

"And meant to be broken."

"Yeah, I guess that's why I got a job."

"I guess maybe I'll just have to solve this one myself."

"I wouldn't try that, if I was you."

"I've got to get these people off my back."

"Sorry, Mike, but all I can give you is the pollice verso."

"Okay, I'll settle for the official version."

"Jeez, okay, just this once. They found semen in the victim's throat."

"Gross. The murderer?"

"No, the semen donor was injured too. Neruda tracked him down, sometimes he does good work, maybe that's why Wayne made sergeant."

"You found the guy?"

"There were two other different blood types at the scene, besides yours."

"Mine?"

"Yeah, Neruda was really trying to nail you."

"I'm AB."

"I know. You're positive, those were both negative."

"So, I'm cleared."

"Neruda still wants to nail you with something."

"Why's he after me?"

"So, Neruda checked the emergency rooms."

"Probably shot himself, to make it look good."

"And there was this graduate student, first degree burns to his right eye, bone splinters in his thigh, and a flesh wound on his left nut."

"Testicle?"

"You know ball, gonad."

"Ouch!"

"That's how I felt. Anyway, the Doc said he was lucky he was coming."

"I always think so."

"No, the Doc said that your balls go up, ascend, and that, if it had been any earlier, the bullet would have taken his left nut right out."

"Double ouch."

"Who asked who?"

"The guy's obviously the murderer."

"Apparently, the bullet entered the back of Gyula's, the victim's head, and came out his mouth. That's why the guys thought it was a suicide."

"The back of his head?"

"They figured he put the gun down his throat and pulled the trigger."

"At least you finally got the guy."

"The angles seem to rule the grad student out."

"He could have held the gun like this."

"Why would anybody do that?"

"Just to throw the cops off the trail."

"Hey, what do I know, I'm just telling what I hear, which I shouldn't be doing anyway. Of course, we'll still hold him for awhile, sweat him, just in case he wants to tell us something, but he's going to walk."

"So who did it?"

"Frankly, I don't know, and I don't care if all those lunatics kill each other. Besides, it's too late for this one. You ever seen a chart of how many murders are solved after 24 hours, I don't mean an arrest, now, just that the dicks know who did it?"

"No."

"Well, it goes like this," Tony raised his flat hand and put it through a swan dive.

"So you're saying there's no chance that they'll find the killer?"

"Count yourself lucky."

"Nobody could call what I'm going through lucky."

"Neruda thinks you had something to do with it."

"In that case, he'll never solve it."

"And the Commander, Lt. Gruber, he thinks it's a Czech assassination, either a new right wing group or even the new government."

"So maybe the FBI or CIA could figure it out."

"He just wants to close the books, make it somebody else's problem."

"He did that already."

"It's not going to work, though. The Alderman and all sorts of community groups are demanding that he take some action."

"But what can he do in Czechoslovakia?"
"I hate politicians, I really do."

Chapter 11

As Mike approached Echo Books, the next morning, he spotted Ernie squatting in front of the store.
"Ernie, what are you doing down there?" Mike asked.
"Cleaning this gang graffiti, what did you think?" Ernie replied.
"Those are pentangles. The witches, I told you about them, they put them there last night."
"They are just another gang trying to harass the local merchants for their juvenile amusement, that's all."
"But it's a sign."
"Of course it is a sign. All the gang graffiti is, it says I was here and I am a moron."
"But it might be useful."
"For what? In my father's day, during the war, every dumb jerk that pulled a prank, wrote 'Killroy was here'. You call it useful, I call it just plain stupid."
"For protection."
"I will never pay any gang for protection. This is not Al Capone's Chicago."
"You think that's what those witches were really after?"

"I am sure, they would call it a donation. But I am not going to play their game. These pentangles or whatever they are called, they are history on my store."

"They may try them again, tonight, you ever think about that?"

"Once they see that I will not put up with any nonsense, and they realize I am far more patient, I am sure their enthusiasm will wane."

"Okay by me."

"Well, get inside, and see if Brian needs any help. This should not take more than another hour, I will be in after that."

"Sure, who are the specials today?"

"The Auteurs du Jour are John Adams and Richard Brinsley Sheridan."

"Sounds pretty dull."

"Well then, wait until tomorrow. You will like tomorrow, tomorrow's Auteurs du Jour are John Keats, Dick Francis and Pee-Wee Herman."

"Dick Francis and Pee-Wee, you're right, I am going to like tomorrow."

"Yes, I thought you would. Now go inside and check with Brian."

"Sure boss."

Mike opened the door and walked into the store. Brian was behind the cash register.

"How's it going Brian, you look tired." Mike said.

"I guess I didn't get much sleep last night." Brian said.

"Yeah, I thought I saw you with Gyula's widow last night."

"Meg, you mean."

"So did you?" Mike asked.

"What?"

"You know, nudge nudge, click click."

"Mike, sometimes you seem really. . . ."

"Yeah, I know, they all say that about me."

"But."

"So did you?"

"If you ask me, she's a sexual bulimic."

"Couldn't get enough of you, huh, and there's a lot of you to get."

"No, I meant in the binge and purge sense."

"She get mad at you?"

"Last night, I was the best thing that ever happened to her. This morning, her worst nightmare. I have no idea what I did or said to make her change mind like that."

"I know what you mean, one day you'll probably get married, the next, some professor gets himself killed, and she won't even talk to you."

"Thanks, but I really doubt they're the same thing."

"Women are women. Of course they're all different, but they're still women."

"It's different."

"Maybe she's schizoid, you know multiple personalities, like Sybil."

"Paranoid, perhaps. She keeps a large hunting knife in her purse and she sleeps with a little gun under her pillow, calls it her baby."

"You weren't snooping in her purse were you?"

"Nope. She told me, that after the L.A. riots and that truck driver, she decided to get something for self-defense." "Well, I'm sure not going to mess with her."

"It's not you she's worried about. You want to work the register?"

"Actually, I'd prefer to shelve and straighten, just in case those witches decide to come back. Kate can take over for you when she comes in."

"Fine with me. She's coming in at two today, she asked Ernie for some extra hours, big date or something. Aside from that, I heard that Ernie talked to Woody."

"Mrs. Mondevi talked to them too, but you never know."

"So you're going to punch them out."

"Oh, the fist. I'm just protecting my on-the-job injury from infection, that's all."

"I wouldn't mention it to Ernie."

"I may as well, go and shelve."

Mike had shelved Literature and Social Science for over an hour and a half, when Kate came in.

"Hey Kate, what are you doing in here so early?" Mike asked.

"I asked Ernie for some extra hours, and he said I could process the rest of the Daedalus order." Kate said.

"Those remainders again. If the new bookstores can't sell them, why should we. You know, what you should do is see if Brian needs a break. He had a hot date with Mrs. Gyula last night, looks like he could use a rest."

"Poor woman, she must be in shock."

"I'd say so, and shocking too."

"He didn't pick her up at your bar?"

"Hard to say who picked up who, but given Brian, I got my suspicions."

"She wasn't drinking was she?"

"Well, yeah, they were at the Roost, what would you expect?" Mike said.

"But that's rape." Kate said.

"No, I think he thought he knew what he was doing."
"I can't believe he actually raped her!"
"Wait a second, they seemed to getting along."
"Brian, Campus Rapist. This goes in the newsletter."
"It's not like I'm making it sound."
"A woman, in a state of profound psychological shock, can not give consent."
"You become a shrink all of a sudden?"
"The alcohol alone. Under the influence of alcohol, nobody can consent to anything and I even think that's the law."
"I guess I've seen my fair share of disagreements in bars. But you're not saying that every time I had a couple beers and Nancy wasn't drinking, that Nancy was a rapist?"
"She was taking advantage of you, but in the law's eyes, in your case, it was probably implied consent."
"That's what I like about beer. I would imply and she would consent."
"Do you want me talk to Nancy about it?"
"I wish you would, I think she thinks I had something to do with Gyula's assassination."
"I'm not surprised."

"Mention Kermit for me."

"The frog?"

Four dark sedans pulled up in front of the store. On either side of the entourage was a police car.

"It looks like we might actually have some customers, probably some foreign diplomats." Kate said.

"And those cops should keep that witch gang away." Mike said.

Ernie rose to great the new customers. His master salesman smile disappeared in a flash. He trailed the three uniformed and four plainclothes policemen into the store, "You mean you're going to close my store, my store, just because of that dumb. . . ." Ernie protested.

"We have a warrant to search the place. We can't search the place with people in it." Sgt. Neruda said.

"So just like that, just because some bozo doesn't know his big toe from his thumb, you are going to put me out of business." Ernie said.

"Pollex." Brian said.

"Rapist." Kate said.

"Thank you, Brian." Ernie said.

"Orders are orders and procedure is procedure." Sgt. Neruda said.

"What are you looking for?"

"I'm not at liberty to say."

"That is just great. You close my store, and you will not even tell me why. Whatever happened to 'due process' and 'unlawful search and seizure'?"

"Take it up with the judge who signed those papers."

"I may very well do that."

"Fine with me. Okay, every body out."

"How long is this highly questionable imposition going to take?"

"We hope to be done today, the guys would like to get home. But, given the number of books you got in this place, it'll probably take two days, maybe three."

"Oh, that is just great. And how am I supposed to make the rent?"

"We don't make the rules, we just enforce them."

"Just tell me what you are looking for and I will find it for you."

"Sorry, but I'm not at liberty to say."

"I bet I know what he's looking for " Mike said.

"You, Mike?" Ernie asked.

"Yeah, I bet they're looking for a small handgun, like the Hlinka Guards use." Mike said.

"Hlinka Guards?" Ernie winced.

"The wise guy's right. We're looking for a .25 auto." Sgt. Neruda said.

"Well, I can tell you right now, there is nothing like that in my store." Ernie said.

"Yeah, if you still think I did it, why don't you check out my place, huh?" Mike asked.

Sgt. Neruda grinned. "That's where we came from. Did you read all those books?" He asked.

"I missed one, but I can't find it."

"That doesn't surprise me."

"I hope you didn't mess up anything."

"It looked like somebody had trashed the place, before we got there."

"Yeah, the cops."

"Get lost."

"Maybe it could stand a little house cleaning." Mike muttered to Kate.

"Excuse me, officer, but would you mind explaining why it has to take so long, and why you're not after rapists?" Kate asked.

"Well, young lady, there is a difference between murder and criminal sexual assault."

"Maybe for men."

"And, you see, a gun as small as a .25, well that could conceivably be concealed in even a large paperback, so we're going to have to check every book, almost, and you got a lot of books in here." Sgt. Neruda said.

"But, that's ridiculous, you don't seriously think that Mike carved out a book?" Kate said.

"That's not my call, but we'll have to rifle through every book."

"For crying out loud, what a waste of the taxpayer's money." Ernie said.

"That's enough. The sooner we get started, the sooner we can leave." Sgt. Neruda said.

"I am not leaving my cash drawer unprotected."

"You stay. We'll need you to unlock things. The rest of you, out."

"Brian, Mike, Kate I guess this means you get a couple days off. I am truly sorry, but with circumstances as they are, I hope you appreciate that the next payroll check will have to be postponed for some time." Ernie said.

"That's okay boss, anything we can do to help?" Brian asked.

"No, I think not."

"When should I come back?" Brian asked.

"I will telephone you."

"How long is this postponement deal going to last?" Mike asked.

"Indefinitely, as far as I can tell." Brian said.

"That's just great." Mike said.

"You sure there's nothing we can do?" Brian asked.
"Finding this silly gun that the officers are looking for, that would help." Ernie said.

Chapter 12

"So, you guys want to head over to Robert's, commiserate and drown some sorrows." Brian asked, as they left the store.
"Authoritarian bastards." Kate said.
"I don't like it neither." Mike said.
"I sure could use a cold one. It's not everyday that the cops close down the place where you work." Brian said.
"They think, just because they have that silly patriarchal costume on, they can do what ever they like." Kate said.
"And, obviously they do." Brian said.
"Rapist." Kate said.
"So it seems to me, we have a consensus here, I like it when folks can get along." Mike said.
"Not only that, but it's Friday, and that means it's Rooster Time." Brian said.
"Yeah, I heard about that, unfortunately, I never seem to get off in time."
"Yep, well then, this is your lucky day."
"Tell me about it."
"What is Rooster Time?" Kate asked.

"Oh, Robin and Robert have this thing, sort of a promotion. You know like a happy hour." Brian said.
"I thought those were illegal in Chicago?"
"My understanding is, only if you advertise them, you know like if you put up a sign or whatever."
"So what is so special about a happy hour?"
"Well, between four and eight, men get two drinks for the price of one."
"No wonder. I suppose the women get one for the price of two."
"No, the drinks are free."
"I'm going to have to tell my friends."
"Check it out, first, believe me, it might not be their cup of tea. Roosters and hens and all that."
"It's not so scary, I was there with Mike on Sunday."
"Yeah, she went dancing with Gyula." Mike said.
"With Zoltan himself?" Brian asked.
"I felt like he was my father, not my father father, but my spiritual father, somehow." Kate said.
"I didn't think he was that old." Mike said.
"I just felt comfortable in his arms." Kate said.
"He's married, or was."
"Dancing." Kate said.
"Still could be dangerous."

"You know why Mennonites don't have sex?" Kate asked.

"I figured they did, but no, why?" Mike asked.

"Because it might lead to dancing."

"I don't get it. Yeah, sure, after the first time, but after that, that's why you go dancing."

"Mike!"

"Let's go see what's going on at the Roost." Brian said.

"I'm curious, myself, about this Rooster thing. Working nights, I've never had a chance to check it out. Roosters and Hens, sounds kind of interesting." Mike said.

"Off, we go then. It runs from 4 until 8." Brian said.

"Talk about perfect timing. That's what you call, serendipity." Mike said.

"The Princes of Serendip, no, we're not looking for anything, so it can't be."

"We're looking for the guys that killed Gyula. We find them, then the cops will open up the store again."

"The Three Musketeers?" Kate suggested.

"More like the Scarecrow, the Tin Man and the Cowardly Lion." Brian said.

"And which one are you?" Kate asked.

"The Cowardly Lion of course. Basically I'd rather not be involved."

"You're not suggesting that I don't have a heart, because if you are. . . ."

"No, no. Nothing of the kind, I just don't see us as musketeers, that's all."

"And here we are, just like I pictured it, you know some day Robin should get her sign fixed." Mike said.

"You can still read it, even if the T doesn't flash." Brian said.

"That's what my point, exactly."

"Time's a wasting."

"You guys go in first." Kate said.

"Scared?" Brian said.

"I just want to establish that I'm with a group, so they don't try to hit on me."

"Wise move. Don't worry though, you got Ken and Bonney behind the bar for protection." Mike said.

"All for one and one for all." Kate said.

"Yeah, Ken I'd like a round of Old Styles for me and my cohort." Mike said.

"Coming right up." Ken said.

"So what do I owe you?" Mike asked.

"Nothing. It's on Mr. Lewis." Ken answered.

"Mr. Lewis?"

"The gentleman at the end of the bar."

"Fergie?"

"Yes, that's what I said. Mr. Fergusson Lewis is buying everyone's drinks."

"But how?"

"With one hundred dollar bills, it's not that hard."

"You guys want to sit at a table or at the bar?" Mike asked

"Bar." Brian said.

"Table." Kate said.

"Bar." Mike said.

"I guess the bar will do." Kate said.

"Thanks for the beer." Brian said.

"No problem, it was free." Mike said.

"Of course, it's always free for women on Fridays." Brian said.

"Fergie bought the round." Mike said.

"He would choose Rooster Time to buy a round, crazy but cheap."

"And he's got some money too."

"What has he done now?"

"Hey, look the gang's all here."

"I suspect all of the suspect are here."

"Most of my friends are here. I know almost everybody in the place."

"That's what I said."
"So, how are we going to solve this thing?"
"What?" Kate asked.
"Professor Gyula's murder." Brian said.
"Well, first we round up the usual suspects and then we ask them the really hard questions." Mike said.
"Like what?" Brian asked.
"I haven't figured that part out yet." Mike said.
"Like who?"
"That part either."
"Well, what do we know so far?" Brian asked.
"He was murdered with a gun." Kate said.
"Very good Kate, that's a start."
"The cops were looking for a small gun weren't they?" Kate asked.
"A .25 auto, I believe." Brian said.
"The kind of gun used by the Hlinka Guards." Mike said.
"Who are the Linked-Up Guards?" Kate asked.
"I never read that anywhere." Brian said.
"I got it from Sylvester." Mike said.
"There's a fine source, if I've ever heard of one." Brian said.
"You knock him, but I think he know's his stuff, least about some things."
"He's an innocent to me." Kate said.

"We can count him out." Brian said.

"You know, I saw Magda at the book sale, you figure, she had anything to do with it?" Mike said.

"Peter's wife? Hum." Brian said.

"I doubt it, they were getting along spectacularly at the Hungarian club." Kate said.

"I thought Nancy was." Mike said.

"She was, but Ms. Prst and Zoltan seemed to have a special connection."

"Doesn't surprise me at all."

"Peter, the jealous husband?" Brian asked.

"He's got a temper, especially when it comes to paying the rent." Mike said.

"He's gets Ernie nervous about the rent too." Brian said.

"Must be that Slovak blood."

"You think maybe he's caught up with those Guards?" Kate asked.

"Either way, he's got to be a prime suspect." Mike said.

"So how do we catch him?" Kate asked.

"There's some other guy, too. Tony was telling me about him yesterday." Mike said.

"Who?" Kate asked.

"I don't know his name, and this is strictly for you guys' ears only, but there was another guy in there with him." Mike said.

"In the stall." Kate said.

"Yep, that's what he said."

"But why, I thought only women went to the women's room together." Kate said.

"They do." Mike said.

"Boys will be boys." Brian said

"Apparently he was loved by all." Mike said.

"Oh." Kate said.

"So did they catch the guy?" Brian asked.

"Tony said they were holding him." Mike said.

"So what are they hassling us for?"

"Maybe he didn't do it."

"Of course he did. He was there, wasn't he?"

"So was Mike, wasn't he?" Kate said.

"Okay, okay, I get your point, so where does that leave us?" Brian said

"I figure we should split up and see what we can find out." Mike said.

"And each of us cross-examine one of the suspects." Brian said.

"Suspects or people that might know something. Look for clues, that kind of thing."

"So who's going to talk to Peter." Brian asked.

"Brian, since you've gotten to know Meg so well, you might question her."

"I'm never going near that woman again, you talk to her."

"I can't, Nancy's at the table, I don't think that I could get the conversation going."

"I'll talk to her." Kate volunteered.

"Good, so Kate's going to join the Peggys. So you want to ask Fergie where all that money came from?" Mike asked Brian.

"That stir-fry for brains, I doubt I could make any sense out of him at all."

"In that case, I guess I'll talk to him."

"So, then, whom do I have the pleasure of talking to?"

"I guess that leaves Pete, unless you can think of someone better than our number one."

"Mike, if I didn't know you better, I could swear you set me up somehow."

"Hey, they were your choices."

"That's what hurts."

"Okay then, let's all split up, it's almost five now, say we meet here again at seven. And be discreet, make it look like a natural accident, that kind of thing."

"Make it six, I'm not sure I can talk to Peter for that long."

"Okay, so how about this, on the hour, we accidentally run into each other by this here cigarette machine. We could talk about the coincidence of it all."

"I don't smoke." Kate said.

"Well pretend that you do, or you're thinking of taking it up, or just that, say you saw something out the window." Mike said.

"Okay, I'll try." Kate said.

"I can't believe we're doing this." Brian said.

"Hey, trust me, I know what I'm doing." Mike said.

Mike walked down the bar and sat next to Fergusson Lewis.

"Hey Fergie, what's up with you these days?" Mike asked.

"Top of the world man, I just got paid and I am doing some celebrating tonight." Fergie said.

"Thanks for buying us a round."

"No problem, the people in here, they take care of me, and when I got some money, I do the same for them."

"Yeah, they're good people, most times."

"You won't find a bar like this anywhere else in Chicago, least I haven't."

"I'm kind of glad it is, otherwise I'd never get to work."

"You still working at the bookstore?"

"Yeah, I talked to you on Wednesday when you came in to use the phone."

"You did? Well these days things change so fast you never know, the depression and all."

"You were playing chess."

"Now, I know you're wrong, Wednesday is not my chess night, Tuesday is, so there is no way I was there on Wednesday, if it was chess night."

"So, what, you think we're in a depression again?"

"History repeats itself."

"Unless you memorize it, as some writer said, probably a history professor."

"You got your go-go 20's and your go-go 80's. You got your wimpy Republican president, that just says it's a minor recession, then and now. And then, you got your silly Democratic presidents who claim they got all the answers, but nothing happens."

"Wait a second here, Roosevelt got us out of the depression, the New Deal and a chicken in every pot."

"Hitler got us out of the depression."

"Hitler, no way man, you got to be kidding."

"Hitler got Germany out of the depression and brought Japan into the war."

"So?"

"The depression wasn't over until Roosevelt cranked up his war machine."

"I thought we were helping out British before that?"

"And the Ford Motor Company was selling tanks to Franco in Spain. No, he didn't want to get himself involved, but Hitler and the Japanese, they forced his hand."

"Why wouldn't he want to get involved, with all the atrocities and all?"

"'Cause big business runs this country, and there's a whole lot of money in selling arms, but people start complaining when their kids get killed, that gets those politicians scared silly. Why do you think they invented the Cold War? So they could sell the guns, the arms and stuff, and it wouldn't be Americans dying. No, it would be Africans, Asians and, actually most of the Americans south of Mexico."

"So you're saying we need World War Three."

"Can't afford it, sure they wouldn't mind killing the kids, if they thought it was necessary and could get it over with before an election, but there's no money left, thanks to Silent Ron."

"You on speed tonight?"

"I'm high on life."

"Yeah, or death, I'm not sure which. Excuse me for a second, I need to get some cigarettes."
"Be my guest, it's your death."
Mike walked to the cigarette machine by the front door. Kate was waiting nervously.
"So, did you learn anything?" Kate asked.
"Nah, just that Fergie's a big Hitler fan. How about yourself?" Mike asked.
"Not much, they seem to vacillate between consoling Meg and criticizing her for sleeping around. Oh, and all sorts of concern about a sick daughter."
"Yeah, I heard."
"I'm not sure I can take much more."
"Hold your horses for just a second, here comes Brian, maybe he's learned something."
"So what have we learned?" Brian asked.
"Meg's daughter is sick, a severe lung infection." Kate said.
"Probably pneumonia." Mike said.
"That's curious." Brian said.
"Fergie thinks Hitler ended the Depression." Mike said.
"That sounds like Fergie."
"How about yourself?" Mike asked.
"Well, it seems that he really hated the guy." Brian answered.

"Could be our man." Mike said.

"His only regret is that he didn't pull the trigger himself."

"He could be trying to throw us off the trail." Kate said.

"Peter? I kind of doubt it, he's pretty much a straight shooter." Brian said.

"I guess you're right." Kate said.

"So, come on guys, go back there and ask some hard questions." Mike said.

"I can't take those women any longer, all they want to talk about is interpersonal relationships. What about politics, what about the global environment? I don't care if the beer is free for 'hens', I'm going home." Kate said.

"Party pooper." Mike said.

"Well, I think I've gotten all I'm going to get out of Peter, I think I'll try my hand at Twisted Sisters." Brian said.

"Yeah, well, I'm going back and ask Fergie some hard questions, and see if I tell you guys anything." Mike said.

Mike turned and headed down the bar. Brian turned to the pinball machine, Kate to the door.

"What do you know about death?" Fergie asked.

"I know the Hlinka guards assassinated that professor over at the U of C." Mike answered.

"Peter told me that nobody in America knew about the organization."

"Yeah, well, this is Hyde Park. There are a lot of fart smellers, in this neighborhood."

"And I'm sure of one of them."

"I wouldn't call myself smart, but I know when something stinks, like where did all those hundred dollar bills come from? Let me ask you that."

"Frankly, it's none of your business. But since you asked, I did a little wrecking job, you know like tearingdown some walls and hauling trash away."

"Sure pays well."

"That's what I did. What they pay me for, that's their problem."

"So what do they think?"

"They seem to have the impression that I had something to do with the demise of a certain professor."

"I wonder what gave them that idea?"

"Well, they did ask me if my services were available in that regard, and the man certainly is dead. And it's not entirely impossible that I might have hinted, ever so slightly, mind you, that there was some connection between the two events."

"So you killed the guy?"

"I never laid my eyes on him. I wouldn't know him from Amos, if he was in here right now."

"What'd they pay you?"

"For the wrecking job, ten grand."

"You better hope they don't find out."

"You're the only one that knows so far, they find out I know who to come looking for."

"I see your point. Excuse me while I get some matches."

"I thought you just bought some cigarettes."

"I did, but I forgot to get some matches."

Mike looked around the bar and realized that Brian had left.

"Here you can have mine, I won't be needing them tonight." Fergie said.

"Thanks, but I wouldn't want to take your last pack of matches." Mike said. "Oh look, Grata just walked in and I wanted to ask him some questions."

"Remember now, Mike, please don't make me kill you, it would ruin my day."

"Mine too. Mum's the word."

"I sure hope so, for you sake, perhaps mine as well."

"Later."

"Later man."

Mike stumbled to the middle of the bar.
"Greetings Occiffer Grata." He said.
   "You spend too much time in here." Tony said.
   "Hey, I'm drinking as fast as I can." Mike said.
   "Your first Rooster Time?"
   "Yeah, how could you tell."
   "I'm a highly trained professional."
   "Then how come you guys haven't caught the guy yet?"
   "I told you, chances are we never will."
   "What about that grad student?"
   "The dicks say the angle's all wrong, no way that soon-to-be-supreme-court-justice could have done it."
   "I thought you said he was a Divinity School student?"
   "Same difference. He kept saying he had this legal right and that moral right, and that this would cry to heaven for justice. I told him, justice was doing okay down here, just as it is. Personally, I couldn't stand that pretty boy."
   "Okay, so how come then, you guys had to come over and close Echo Books, I mean come on, my rent is due on Sunday."
   "I told you I hated politicians."
   "So?"

"Your Alderman, responding to pressure from certain community groups, which will remain nameless, put pressure on the Commander to do something visible."

"But I thought, you said, he thought it was a European thing?"

"He does, but when you get up that high up, you have got to know which way the wind blows."

"Yeah, well, it stinks in here."

"Mike, it's after midnight, don't you think it's time?"

"Just a few more one or two questions, I don't have to work tomorrow, but I don't want to have to make that an everyday thing."

"Shoot."

"Okay, you're saying that the only reason that you guys checked out my place and then closed Echo was because of the Alderman wanted something done."

"Have you seen all the stop signs in the Fifth Ward, believe me it happens."

"But you guys claimed you was looking for gun, a .25 I believe, well I know who you should be asking."

"Leave the police work to the professionals."

"Lot of good that would do me. You want to find a gun, ask Prst about that gun he bought for

Magda, a .25 I believe, and while you're at it, ask the widow about that gun she keeps under her pillow."

Chapter 13

At five o'clock, Mike walked into Robert's Roost with his fishing gear. He leaned the rod against the wall and sat in the first stool by the door.
"Hi Robin." Mike said.
"Hello there Mike, long time no see. What can I get you? An Old Style perhaps?" Robin said.
"Yeah, that would be great."
"We hardly ever see you around here these days."
"Yeah, well I've been working at the bookstore, afternoons and evenings, so I don't get much chance to get here early." Mike said.
"Just be careful, we don't want anything to happen to you." Robin said.
"Don't worry I've been working there for over a year and a half."
"Is that the University Bookstore?"
"Nah, Echo Books over on 53rd by Mr. G's."
"Nevertheless."
"Where's Ken, anyhow?"

"Kenji doesn't work on weekends. Robert's not feeling well, so I'll take care of things until Kazimir arrives at seven."

"You should have called Nancy."

"I did, but she said, regretfully, she was entertaining a gentleman."

"I should say that it's regretful. I mean, stranding a woman in her sixties to run the bar all by herself."

"You are too kind."

"Seriously."

"So, I see, you were out fishing today."

"Yeah, sometimes on Saturdays, I like to go out there and cast for a while. Get my mind off of things."

"Catch much?"

"Nah, the only thing I catch is snags."

"I overheard a customer once, say that those are the hardest fish to catch, they put up such a fight."

"Almost impossible, and ugly as sin too, if you do."

"What do you do?"

"I play with it for five minutes and see if it'll let go of the lure. After that, if it doesn't, that means I got to cut the line."

"Sounds like a terrible waste."

"Yeah, lures do get expensive, especially those brand names, that's why I try to make my own."
"I mean, that poor fish, with that hook caught in it's throat, it's going to starve to death."
"Well, I got a frog in mine or, maybe I'm dying of thirst."
"Another Old Style coming right up, Sir!"
Kaz lumbered into the bar and sat next to Mike.
"Robin has been treating you well I trust?" Kaz said.
"Like I was the only guy in the place." Mike said.
"It starts slow on Saturdays."
"I thought you got on at seven?"
"I do, but I like coming in early to see what kind of, let us say, characters are in the place."
"No trouble-makers tonight. Just me, the Peggys at their table, and Meg, the widow over at the other end."
"So far so good."
Robin returned with a beer, "You have to pay for that, young man."
"Sorry Robin, take it out of here." Mike said.
"So what's news, bar-wise?" Kaz asked Robin.
"They gave us those short-necked non-returnable Old Style bottles again." Robin said.

"Oh no, I'm going to miss again for sure." Mike said.

"Again?" Robin said.

"Apparently." Kaz said.

"My mind knows the exact distance for hand to mouth coordination when it comes to long neck Old Styles." Mike said.

"You know, we're going to have to do something about it, give me a couple days to come up with a plan." Kaz said to Robin.

"I think I'll pay that driver cash next time, you know how he hates that." Robin answered.

"That'll probably work."

"Don't blame me if I make a mess." Mike said.

"Be a dear and do try to be careful." Robin said.

"You do it on my shift, you clean it on my shift." Kaz said and asked Robin, "Anything else?"

"Well, I believe the Prsts were arrested, Wayne was in for lunch." Robin answered.

"That's terrible, they were pretty regular." Kaz said.

"I'm going to miss them, the misses especially, her husband on the other hand." Robin said.

"I knew it, I knew it was them." Mike said.

"Wait until Tony comes in, then we'll see what he says." Kaz said.

"So, they finally caught them, and just in time." Mike said.

"I don't know what you're talking about young man." Robin said.

"I think it's about Mr. and Mrs. Prst." Kaz said.

"It's a long story, what it boils down to is this, I don't have to pay the rent tomorrow." Mike explained.

"So what, tomorrow's Sunday." Kaz said.

"Well I'm a little short on funds right now, and Prst, he works seven days a week, and he knows where to find me, anyhow." Mike said.

"Right."

"Besides, with the bookstore open again, maybe Ernie would spring for a loan."

"Robin, do you know why the Prsts were arrested?" Kaz asked.

"He never said they were arrested. Wayne said something about finding the gun they were looking for, and then they took them in. I can put two and two together." Robin said.

"So he didn't exactly say they did it. Nothing like that?" Kaz asked.

"If you don't believe me, why don't you just talk to Mike here, I have other customers to take care of, you know!" Robin said.

"I know what you think." Kaz said to Mike.

"It's got to be them, all the clues point in their direction." Mike said.

"It doesn't sound like Petr to me."

"Maybe it was his wife Magda, maybe she was setting him up or something. I'm just glad it's over with that's all."

"Right." Kaz said and glanced at the fishing rod, "I see you've been fishing again."

"In the rocks, over by 51st Street."

"Floyd told me he saw you out there once."

"Who's Floyd?"

"Floyd Pinkerton, I thought you knew him?"

"You must mean Mr. Pink, yeah, he's always out there, catches about as much as I do, be my guess."

"Is it true you take fried chicken and a six pack of Old Style with you, when you go?"

"He said that?"

"Who else could come up with something like that?"

"Pete, maybe. But, I might as well, I never catch anything besides a cold."

"A fish with the fish."

"Like I like to say, if you can't catch them, join them."

Kaz closed his eyes and shook his head slowly, "Remind me sometime, why I didn't finish my dissertation."

"I thought you had."

"No, I got through 300 pages, and then my advisor said I needed to change direction."

"What kind of jerk would do something like that?"

"He was at the U of C."

"So, I guess you did change direction, after all."

"What's so wrong with a history of Hyde Park, I mean come on, it has a lot to say about how this city grew up, development, that sort of thing."

"The guy didn't like Hyde Park, be my guess."

"No, and I should have realized that from the beginning, he's one of those destructuralists. Then again, maybe I was too young to realize the trouble I was getting myself into."

"You and me both."

"How so?"

"That Gyula guy, he was one of those destruction guys, and ever since he died, Nancy won't talk to me."

"Sometimes it's for the best."

"Like your Ph.D., or maybe you're becoming a destructionist yourself."

"Fat chance."

"So what are the chances of me getting Nancy back?"

"Same as my Ph.D."

"Once she learns about the Prsts, I'm home free."

"Somehow, I suspect not, Pally." Kaz said.

Mel and Nancy wheeled into the bar on rollerblades. Sweat ran down the creases of their smiles, as they beamed at each other. They skated to the farthest table. Mel wiped and fanned his brow with the bottom of his T-Shirt. Nancy pretended she didn't notice his rippled stomach.

"Frankly, I'd say you don't stand a chance." Kaz said.

"Oh yeah, just wait and see, two can play this game." Mike said.

"Just don't start anything." Kaz said.

"I won't start nothing that I can't finish. Trust me." Mike said.

"I know you."

"Watch, you'll see."

"Good luck Pally."

"Luck's got nothing to do with it."

Mike ambled down the bar and tried not to look to his left at the tables. He stopped at the end of the bar.

Rule of Thumb

"Ah, excuse me, is this seat taken?" Mike asked.

"I don't see anybody sitting in it do you?" Meg answered.

"Just me, myself and I." Mike said.

"I hope you have fun talking with yourselves." Meg said.

"Actually, I wanted to express my deep regrets about your recent loss."

"Who?"

"I thought the famous Zoltan Gyula was your husband."

"He used to be."

"Sorry, I mean, being a widow, that's got to be rough."

"Life, holds so many surprises."

"Like what?"

"How old are you?"

"28."

"Don't turn forty."

"I'll try not to."

"Did anyone ever tell you, how incredibly sexy your hands are?"

"Not till now."

"Oh, your thumb, it's short."

"So?"

"It is just so terribly sexy, it means your not one of those bossy types, ... like my ex-husband."
"I guess."
"And it's so straight and thick."
"That's what Nancy said."
"Who is this Nancy, that knows you so well?"
"My ex-wife."
"I knew we had a lot in common."
"She thought I was too stubborn."
"Aren't we all sometimes. But you're obviously not, your thumb is too short."
"I just know what makes me mad."
"With a thumb as thick and straight as yours, you should use intuition to solve any difficulties."
"I'm done intuiting anything."
"Why?"
"I know you've had it rough, but, you know, sometimes it rubs off on other people."
"Tell me about it."
"That's what I'm doing."
"You're what?"
"It's been a rough week, first the cops think I killed your husband, and then those witches, and the --- I don't know."
"I'm sure that you didn't."
"Thanks for the vote of confidence."

"You know, it's terrible Zolly died, but all this fuss. It had to be either the STB or the Hlinkas, and I doubt your Chicago police will ever find them."

"You know about them too?"

"Doesn't everybody, after all the STB doesn't just do assassinations."

"Sylvester said it was the SIS."

"I don't care what they're calling themselves, these days, it's got to be them."

"History memorizes itself, as they say." Mike said.

"As attractive as I might find you, I'm not following."

"Well, I was thinking. Being Halloween and all, there's a party over at Omega Alpha Lambda. We could check out Prairie City, and then see what the Owls are up to."

"Owls?"

"Check out the party over at WAL, which just happens to be right next door."

"It sounds wonderful. Zolly had such wonderful things to say about that bookstore."

"Yeah, it's okay. But the sorority, that's something else."

"Do you think there will be any men there?"

"Usually at those Greek parties, they've got more men than women, but being a sorority and all, I'd say by the rule of thumb, it should be about fifty-fifty."
"Sounds perfect."
"You know, you have nice looking fingers yourself, sort of elegant, you know, long and slender."
"It means I'm good at giving directions."
"Long fingers?"
"A long thumb."
"It curves in, too."
"That means I make thoughtful decisions."
"I guess you've had to make a lot of those these days."
"Yes, Alecto, Alex, my two-year old, has been ill for quite some time."
"I heard she had pneumonia or something."
"Yes, she did, she's always been a sickly child."
"But they cured it."
"For the time being. Can I trust you to keep a secret?"
"Yeah, sure. Cross my heart and hope to die, stick a needle in my eye."
"The doctors told me that my baby has AIDS."
"It can't be true, she's too young."
"They called it 'vertical transmission'."

"I never heard of anyone getting it vertical. Horizontal, now...."
"I think they mean in terms of generations."
"So vertical would mean...."
"They told me she got it from me, that I am HIV positive."
"I'm sorry."
"It's not your fault."
"I know, but."
"It's almost funny, I saved myself for my wedding night, and that's the thanks I get."
"Did you?"
"I was so furious, when they told me. I immediately flew out here, and wouldn't you know it."
"Flagrante delicto."
"I was on fire. I finally had Zolly under my thumb, and my baby blew him a kiss."
"Wow."
"Funny, I don't remember pulling the trigger."
"Sounds like justifiable homicide to me."
"That's what the girls said."
"Girls?"
"Gretchen, Rita and Marjorie."
"Oh, the Peggys."
"And a brunette, Nan."
"Nancy knows?"

"Why yes, don't tell me that was your ex-wife, she's cute."

"I won't, but I'll tell you one thing, your secret's safe with me."

"Thank you."

"I was getting tired of working at the bookstore, anyhow."

"I do apologize for the trouble I've caused you."

"Call it serendipity."

"Are we still on for the party?"

"Sure, why not, it's not every day that a guy gets to take an attractive widow to the owls."

Mike noticed Tony come into the bar, followed by Neruda. Another cop stayed by the front door. Mike turned and saw another cop in the hall by the back door.

"Congratulations, there, Mike, you snagged yourself the murderer. Personally, I didn't think you knew what you were doing. Just goes to show." Tony said.

Meg glared at Mike.

"Yeah, I heard you guys arrested the Prsts." Mike said.

"Them too. I ran your idea about the guns past Wayne, and he didn't want to, but he checked it out." Tony said.

"That's how you caught Magda." Mike said.
"That's how we caught your lady friend here."
"Why would she?"
"Lab guys matched up her gun."
"You bastard." Meg snarled.

Meg reached into her purse, grabbed her knife and swung at Mike. The bar exploded with gun shots. Tony's bullet hit Meg's ring finger and sent the knife flying. The slug from Neruda's gun caught her in the nose. Blood and brains splattered the shattered mirror behind the bar. Mike wiped the drops off his forehead and watched the fine pink mist of miasma drift across the bar.